Cloudy Witness

Cloudy Witness

Blessedly Assured

Janette Jones

WestBow
PRESS
A DIVISION OF THOMAS NELSON

WestBow Press books may be ordered through booksellers or by contacting:

WestBow Press
A Division of Thomas Nelson
1663 Liberty Drive
Bloomington, IN 47403
www.westbowpress.com
1-(866) 928-1240

Biblical references unless otherwise posted were taken from
The New International Version Bible
The New Analytical Reference Bible
The Recovery Version Bible

Jezebel Stereotype Papers
David Pilgrim
Jim Crow Museum - Ferris State University
Permission granted

Jezebel in Our Society: webpage of Albatrus

Golf slogan taken from SHOUT SLOGANS

ISBN: 978-1-4497-5206-4 (sc)
ISBN: 978-1-4497-5205-7 (hc)
ISBN: 978-1-4497-5207-1 (e)
Library of Congress Control Number: 2012908671

Printed in the United States of America

WestBow Press rev. date: 08/09/2012

As a tribute to all that is holy, this book is dedicated to those who will hear what the Spirit is saying.

Praise God from whom all blessings flow, and for being my driving force. All honor and all glory belong to Him.

I especially owe my thanks and gratitude to all the former casts of Sistah-Girl.

And most importantly, a special thank you to my family, my husband Jerry, sons, Tee and Jeremy, and my daughter Leslie for their loving support.

Thank you to my cousin Samuel Lofton for his valuable editorial input.

I especially wish to thank my not so little brother, Samuel Jones for readily grasping my vision from the start. Your belief in me and my abilities never wavered.

Thank you to all my friends for the encouragement and the support through the years.

Preface

It has taken nearly a year to write this book, but I was being prepared for it for much longer. I gave myself away unto the Holy Spirit in many late hours, in order to bring this awe inspiring work of Christian fiction to fruition.

Cloudy Witness derived from a night vision, whereby Hebrews 12:1 NIV was made manifest to the author.

"Therefore, since we are surrounded by such a great cloud of witnesses, let us put off everything that so easily entangles, and let us run with patience this race marked out for us."

What do you suppose your reaction would be if given the opportunity to interact with the likes of the first family, Adam and Eve?

Cloudy Witness takes you into a world of biblical personalities whose lives intercept the day to day activity of seven unsuspecting friends.

Etta Mae and Donnie Smith, Tonika and Josh Gibbons, Delilah and Damien Whitman, along with Stephanie Willis, all face life altering encounters.

Two of which even hold audience with a lone figure clothe in white.

Along with the saints of old, we're also encompassed about by evil entities as well. In this moving drama, anticipate displays of anger, defiant attitudes, as well as rejoicing, as the fictive characters interact with the likes of Jezebel and the wife of Potiphar.

This literary work is comprised of fictional characters taken from *Sistah-Girl* and *Brotha-Man,* two stage productions written by the author.

Sistah-Girl is an epic adaptation of twelve biblical women's impact on the lives of fictional modern day personalities.

It had its first successful run in 2002, and again in 2005 as *Sistah-Girl Revisited. Sistah-Girl Now & Again* was presented in 2008 as a tribute to a beloved, deceased cast member. Each time receiving rave reviews from city-wide audiences.

Brotha-Man affords the biblical characters of Adam and Eve the opportunity to share their side of their story and was written in 2006.

As a disclaimer, this work of fiction is not intended to diminish the validity of the Holy Scriptures from which references were taken.

Neither was it written in a judgmental viewpoint of one's life choices. For we rejoice in knowing our Lord and Savior, Jesus the Christ does not judge us before we obtain His grace and His mercy.

After reading *Cloudy Witness,* the reader may be found conducting an in-depth interrogation of their own spiritual commitment.

Soul searching questions that may arise are: Would I be able to cope with that life shattering crisis if I found myself in the same situation? Do I have the blessed assurance I've run with patience this earthly race? Or am I; *"Looking unto Jesus, the author and finisher of my faith?"* Heb. 12:2a NIV

These and perhaps other questions may only be answered through the psalm of King David.

"Search me, O' God, and know my heart; test me and know my anxious thoughts."

Psalm 139:23 NIV

Chapter One

The discomposed wife walked out of her bedroom fully knowing her five year marriage was now over. The woman's blossoming beauty was overshadowed this morning by a downtrodden spirit. Long tapered fingers raked through tousled hair twirling the frazzled ends around themselves.

Tonika Gibbons usually wore her heavy locks pulled back in a bouncing ponytail. The mocha complexioned, bi-racial 5'10"thirty-nineyear old was the only child of a black army sergeant father and a German mother.

When her father's tour of duty in Germany had ended, the family had made their home in Fayetteburg, North Carolina where she had attended high school, excelling in her classes.

Tonika had attended Fayetteburg State University, but had dropped out during her sophomore year, opting instead to make a career in real-estate.

She had met and married Jamal Tulufano, an American Samoan, after a year's courtship. The adorable couple had moved to New Jersey behind Jamal's construction job. The marriage, unfortunately, had only lasted four years.

Tonika no longer viewed the world through rose colored glasses, but had simply resolved to take life one day at a time.

A year or so after her divorce she had met and married a tall, handsome, aspiring entrepreneur by the name of Josh Gibbons.

Josh's number one priority in life was to be the owner of a lucrative business.

Before he and Tonika married, he'd tried his hand at bringing his dream to fruition, only to fall prey to a number of get-rich-quick schemes.

His confidence had been boosted the day he'd opened JG's Trendy Duds. The hip-hop clothing store had been located on the first floor of the Shady Brooks Mall, and in the beginning had been an enormous success.

But, unfortunately, this venture too, had proven unprofitable as time went on. The dated inventory hadn't been able to keep pace with the trendy, hip hop styles of teenage mind-sets.

After he'd fallen behind on his monthly rental fee and other business expenditures the store had folded.

The adamant dreamer, equipped with strong determination, had vowed he would someday become the successful entrepreneur he longed to be.

This morning, as time would have it, the scorned inamorata found herself on the short end of yet another marital relationship gone sour.

She grabbed a tissue from the marble kitchen counter and forcibly blew her high-bridged nose that had been rubbed raw after a night of weeping.

The scene that had led to Josh storming out of the house with his suitcase that morning resurfaced in her thoughts.

After the biggest argument of their marriage, she had gotten up, and had locked the bedroom door when she'd heard his car pull into the drive-way, extremely late. Josh had slept on the couch.

The incident that had led up to all the drama had all started when he'd returned home from work. Josh hadn't noticed the folded paper that had fallen from his shirt pocket while he hastily discarded his clothing.

Tonika had sauntered into the bedroom hoping to set their date-night in motion.

"Hey, babe . . . what 'a ya say the three of us go out to a movie tonight after dinner?"

The folded sheet of paper lying on the floor had caught her eye. As she had bent to pick it up, a whiff of perfume had caused her to sneeze. She had unfolded the paper and had feverishly scanned the contents.

"What the hell?"

She could hardly believe her eyes. It felt as if breath had been knocked out of her.

"O, my God!"

The sound of the shower could be heard through the bathroom door.

The scorned woman had burst into the steamy bathroom, and in a quick swoop had angrily thrown back the shower curtain.

"What-da? Hey! Tonika what are you doing?" Josh had exclaimed.

"What in the hell is this?" She had demanded, holding the crunched paper in her fist.

Josh had grabbed for a towel before stepping out of the shower.

Tonika had begun to read the contents of the note with wrathful fervor.

"I'm still basking in the glow of our love from our night together. I can't wait to be with you again. Hurry back, lover boy."

He had reached for the critical evidence, but she had backed out of his reach. Tonika had thrown the crumpled paper in his face and had stormed out of the bathroom.

The realization of knowing he had been caught red handed took a while to sink in. Finally, he had concluded it was pointless to offer any form of explanation.

Josh had shrugged his shoulders in defeat. If the truth be told, he had actually found the disclosure of the matter a blessed relief. He had contemplated putting an end to their marital facade for some time.

Admittedly, the endless amount of time his wife spent with their neighbor, a devout Christian from across the street, had left him with a void feeling.

He had thought of how increasingly disheartened he had become lately in their intimate relationship, but hadn't known how to approach the matter of separating.

He hadn't known exactly when the luster had left, but only knew he no longer felt the way he once had.

There had been a time when the daring lioness' uninhibited prowess in the boudoir had left little room for complaint for the virile stud muffin.

"Well . . . as fate would have it, no better time than now." The exposed cheater had thought.

He couldn't help but reflect on how he had reached this point in his life.

After the loss of his last business venture, his only other option had been to return to the ineffective work-force.

The housing market had taken a downward turn, which left Tonika's contribution to their household finances very limited.

He had soon gained employment at the Enterprise Telemarketing

Corporation (ETC) as a sales rep and had quickly become a top salesman.

Karla Jordan, an upwardly mobile senior accountant for the firm, three years Josh's junior, had unexpectedly captured his interest.

A picture of beauty with a drop-dead figure, and a head of highlighted bouncy curls had sashayed into the company's cafeteria one day.

The above-the-knee skin tight periwinkle pencil skirt had held Josh mesmerized. A glimpse of ample breast could be seen through the peek-a-boo hole in the multi colored, form fitting top.

The grilled chicken breast sandwich had lain untouched as his eyes had followed her every move. Their eyes had briefly met.

"Man, look at that! Who does *that* belong to?"

Josh had said to Steven Cox, a co-worker who shared the adjacent cubicle.

Steven's eyes had followed the salivating man's gaze, but had quickly dropped. He had issued a strict warning.

"Stay away from that, dude. You don't want to mess with her, that's 'Miss Fire Starter,' she's bad news."

"Oh, is that right?"

Steven's warning had only heightened Josh's interest.

"In other words, don't ignite the kindling, you may get scorched. You catch my drift? Especially, with you being a married man and all."

Josh had stopped listening after hearing fire starter. He felt as if he just had to get to know the beguiling temptress better.

His feet had propelled him to rise, leaving the co-worker with a startled look. Josh made his way out of the cafeteria and had hesitantly approached Karla on the veranda.

"Excuse me, but i-is this seat taken?"

Karla ran her eyes up and down the length of the magnificent specimen that stood before her.

She liked what she saw. Sizing up her prey, she'd quickly made a mental note of the platinum wedding band on his left finger and had mischievously smiled. The wedding band made no difference to the well-known home wrecker.

"It will be . . . once you sit down, First Sergeant." She'd said, smiling seductively.

The smooth skinned six-foot hunk standing timidly before her reminded Karla of a favorite television commercial that had once aired.

A ranked army officer was always greeted by his troops with a "Good morning, First Sergeant."

Karla and her rowdy girlfriends had forever been infatuated with the handsome male figure featured in the popular commercial.

To which point, she would often size up all unsuspecting dating prospects to his likeness. Needless to say, Josh had been warmly received, and the amorous flame had been ignited.

Josh brought his thoughts back to the moment at hand. The six-month tryst with Karla had now been exposed, thanks to a little white note. It had never been his intention for his wife to find out about his extra marital affair, especially in such a destructive way.

His mind had gone back to the initial conversation he'd had with the co-worker. Fire Starter had been what he had called her.

"That she was and then some!"

An all-knowing smile had spread across his face at the recollection of their ravaged lovemaking. Karla had slipped the note into his shirt pocket as she came up behind his chair.

She had allowed his head to rest upon her breasts before stealing away, with a knowing grin on her face. The unexpected gesture had caused the phone to fall from the surprised lover's hand.

After retrieving the fallen receiver, he had hastily offered the unfortunate customer at the other end a hurried apology. The affectionate display had not been lost on Steven, or any of the other co-workers.

The love-struck buck had meant to destroy the note after reading it, but he had been accosted by Steven, who had leaned over from his cubicle.

"I saw that . . . man just be careful, please!" He had cautiously said. "Don't say I didn't warn you."

"That bloke is surely asking for trouble."

Steven had sternly said to Stephanie Willis, his co-worker seated across from him.

"He sure is because I know his wife!"

Stephanie had eagerly awaited the opportunity to share the juicy gossip with her lunch buddies.

"What to do, what to do . . ." Josh had thought to himself as he dried the beads of water from his glistening torso. The only thing to do now he had concluded was to go out and be confronted by the pissed off hornet.

Just the thought of the imminent confrontation had caused drops of sweat to trickle down his wet brow.

In the bedroom, uncontrollable tears had run down the betrayed woman's face as she sat shivering in the evening coolness. She had suddenly flinched when the billowing curtains brushed against her leg causing goosebumps.

Finally, what seemed to her like an eternity, the door to the bathroom had hesitantly opened. Josh had stood there wrapped in a towel.

At the sound of the opening door, the instinct of attack had over taken the 'screaming banshee.' She had sprung up from the bed with arms flailing, and had yelled at the top of her lungs.

"Who is she? You cheating bastard! And how could you do this to me?"

"Stop it Toni! Now, I'm warning you; you don't want to do this."

Josh had tried to catch a hold of the flailing arms and had drastically tried to deflect the wild blows.

Smaaack

The sound had echoed. She had swung her fist once again and had slapped the traitor with an open hand across his wet face.

His face had burned from the sting of the blow. He had pushed the out of control dynamo down onto the bed, but she'd jumped up once again.

"Damn it, woman, stop it, I said!"

He had somehow managed to turn her taut body around with her arms crisscrossed, and had held on tightly.

The room had been filled with both their heavy breathing. She had frantically squirmed while trying to loosen the tight grip he had on her wrists.

"Let me go you traitor, get off me!" She had muttered through clenched teeth, steadily squirming.

"I mean it; let me go and don't you ever touch me again!"

"Okay, okay . . . . I'm going to let go of you, but damn it, don't start swinging at me again, now I mean it!"

He had given her a slight shove and had stepped back, which had caused her to lose her balance. She had corrected her footing and had rubbed her wrist to regain circulation.

"Well . . . I'm listening." She had said to Josh in between deep, wrenching breaths.

The muddled betrayer of his marriage vows had taken a seat in the nearby Parson's chair. Josh had grasped his lowered head in his hands and had loudly sighed. Tonika, with her arms folded, had defiantly continued to stand.

"Tonika . . . now look." Josh had released a long sigh. "I'm sorry . . . okay? But it's just not working out, and it hasn't been for a very long time." He looked forlornly at his sobbing wife. "And you know for yourself it hasn't; so why fool ourselves?"

The broken-hearted woman hadn't bothered to wipe away the hot, salty tears that had rolled down her face.

"I've been meaning to tell you, but I just couldn't seem to find the right time." Josh had gone on to say. "But . . . now that you know; you know. It's just that simple."

The fuming woman had shifted her weight from one foot to the other. It had been all she could do not to land another well deserving blow.

"If it makes you feel any better, I'll be out of your hair by tomorrow morning. Just give me time to gather all my things."

He had gone over to his chest of drawers. The last remark, however, hadn't sat well with the discarded home-maker. She had stormed over behind him and had forcibly spun the culpable traitor around.

"Oh! So it's just that simple, huh? And just how are you going to fix your *damn* mouth to say, it's just that simple?

There's nothing simple about any of this bull! As a matter of fact, why don't you just get all your punk trash, and get out right now!" She had stomped her foot.

"Just get the hell out!"

Tonika had brushed the startled man aside and had grabbed neatly folded clothes from a drawer, and had thrown them all into the hallway.

"I'm sick of you, and I don't want to see your ugly face around here ever again!"

"Damn it girl! You didn't have to do all that." Josh had said, as he bent to retrieve his favorite football jersey and blue jeans.

"I said I was sorry, now back off!"

"You're sorry? Is that all you can fix your damn mouth to say to me; you're sorry?"

It felt as if the wind had been knocked out of her, she had sat down on the bed and had begun to weep once again.

Josh had merely shrugged his shoulders and had returned to the task of locating the articles of clothing.

After dressing, he had grabbed his car keys and had left the room, leaving behind a duped victim.

"I'm coming back in the morning to get my things." He had yelled from the kitchen.

The exhausted, deserted woman had fallen back on the bed and had sobbed a river of tears.

Bewildered, she'd wondered just how so much water could come from one person. She had rolled over and had beaten the pillow with her fist.

"Damn you woman, whoever you are; damn, damn, damn you!"

Tonika reasoned she would go over to her friend's house tomorrow and have a good cry on her shoulder.

Maybe she could help make sense of everything. She had cried herself to sleep.

The next morning, she lay motionless while sunlight flowed into the room. Tonika reflected on the previous day's occurrence. All she knew was that she had given their marriage her full devotion for the past five years.

She had noticed a change come over him. He had become abstractedly distant. There had been the times he arrived home late from work without bothering to offer any explanation.

She remembered how he had once copped an attitude with her about the amount of time she spent in Bible study and church with Etta Mae. She had simply chalked it up as that being the reason.

No doubt, she had grown spiritually under her friend's tutelage. Her parents' free-will attitude had allowed her to choose whether or not she'd wanted to practice any form of religion while growing up. It had also been the same for Josh.

Tonika was overcome with a sense of foreboding. Just the thought of becoming a single parent once again was frightening. Her mind retreated to her first marriage, and how she and Jamal had greatly anticipated having a brood of kids.

They had wanted at least two boys and two girls. After trying for some time, the jubilant couple had learned Ashad, their first child, would soon become 'big brother' to a little sister.

Her name was to have been Adrika. The two children would've been a year apart in age. However, the couple's joy had been short lived when she had suffered a miscarriage in the third trimester. This was due largely to a sub-mucosal fibroid tumor that had grown along with the baby inside her uterus.

Tonika had awakened one night from a fitful sleep to find her bed linen soaked with blood. Jamal had rushed her to the emergency room. There, they had soon learned the placenta had separated from her uterine wall. Their infant daughter had succumbed in the womb from the lack of oxygen.

She had received two blood transfusions after having become chronically anemic. The AIDS scare was in full bloom at the time, so the thought of having to receive a stranger's blood had left her with frayed nerves. She had watched with dismay as the red life-giving substance had crept slowly down the tube and into her arm.

After the little coffin was interred, life in their household had gone downhill from there. Jamal had suffered with a bout of depression and never recovered from their loss. Tonika had often wondered if he had somehow blamed her. Then one day, unexpectedly, he just up and left.

Jamal's departure had left her in a terrible state of mind, along with a financial bind. Work as a real estate agent had proven to be an unprofitable venture in the days of economic recession. No one was buying, and no one was selling.

But through it all she had made it, even as her savings had slowly dwindled. Thank God, for her sweet, kind neighbors. She would be forever grateful to Donnie and Etta Mae Smith. They'd watched two-year old Ashad nearly every other night for years while she had moonlighted as a hostess at a swank restaurant.

She had met Josh at that same restaurant. He'd been everything she'd been looking for in a marriage partner. Ashad finally had a father figure in his life.

"Well . . . here goes, there's no use hoping the cheat will stick around after this."

The void his infidelity had caused in their relationship was much too vast to mend.

"No use in my hanging on to wishful thinking."

Tonika resolved that she would allow the cheater to return and gather his belongings. It was mostly clothes anyways. Thankfully, her home had already been established when they'd married.

Josh had come into the relationship with nothing more than his treasured classic red Trans Am. Yet, he had shared his limited finances unselfishly. All in all, he had more than adequately provided for their family.

Chapter Two

"**A**ngels! O, my God! The sky is full of angels! A-and there's someone sitting on a throne! My Lord is that . . . ?"

The vision vanished just as quickly as it manifested. Her sleep filled eyes flew open.

"No-oo! It mustn't end. It was too beautiful!"

The fifty-something registered nurse with skin the tone of pure cocoa, commanded her ample body to lie still, trying to comprehend it all.

"Amid disquieting dreams in the night..." Mm mm, okay Job, I'm with you on that one. Apparently, God will speak through a dream, in a vision of the night just like you said.

Etta Mae Smith's mind was bombarded with all sorts of possibilities.

"Wait!" A keen thought had suddenly registered.

She recalled reading how a prophet had once saw 'ten foot' angels come through his church walls. Heck, according to that prophet, even Jesus had made an appearance, and had walked the church isles.

"Maybe something supernatural will happen today. Come

to think of it, Eliphaz did have an unnatural visitor." Etta Mae chuckled.

Shucks you never know. But Lord help me. I don't know what I'd do if that should happen. I'd probably be like Job's friend, all the hair on my body might stand on end. One thing for sure, man definitely can't put our God in a box.

To say He speaks this way, or He does things that way is questionable, because "the Almighty" definitely does what He desires to do, when He desires to do, and how He desires to do, because He is Sovereign!"

A hint of daylight eluded the corners of the 'light blocker' shades on the double windows. Enough to allow her groggy eyes to focus on the clothing scattered around the room.

The disheveled appearance of the room was the result of her husband's frantic search for an article of clothing he somehow convinced himself he desperately needs.

"Darn, the sun is up already. The question is, am I ready to meet this day?"

"One thing for sure, with daylight saving time your day begins bright and early, whether you're ready to face it or not. Where does man get off messing with time anyway?"

Etta Mae allowed a huge sigh to escape her lips as her hand felt the space next to her. It was empty. She rose on one elbow and looked inquiringly at the vacant spot.

"Good grief!"

She made quick work of tucking an annoying wisp of hair that had fallen from under her silk night cap.

"Where's that man, and what time is it getting to be anyhow?"

She threw both legs over the side of the bed and glanced at the clock on the night stand.

"It's only six o'clock in the morning? *Humph*, now I know that fool can't already be on that darn golf course."

She, of course, was referring to her husband of thirty-eight years, Donnie Leroy Smith.

"I hate to say it, but the love that man has for that blessed game borders on obsession."

"Shucks, come to think of it, football widows don't have anything on me."

An annoying ache in her left shoulder caused her considerable discomfort. She rotated the shoulder in a circular motion hoping to relieve the stiffness.

The dull ache resulted from a shoulder impingement brought on by a bursitis flare up.

The flare-ups seemed to be occurring more frequently. Sometimes, just lying on her right side offered a bit of welcomed relief.

There had been a time she'd welcomed having the full range of the bed, but not this morning; pain or no pain, she needed to share her experience.

Although, it wasn't as if the old man could offer any semblance of an interpretation, but just being able to share it with him would have made the dream . . . correction, vision more surreal.

"Hey babe . . ." Donnie had entered the bedroom scratching his head.

Her husband's sudden appearance had caused her to jump, she clutched at her chest.

"Donnie! You scared the heck out of me!"

"Sorry, I didn't mean to." He was startled by her sudden reaction.

"I thought you were on the ninth hole by now."

"Now, why would you think that? You know I don't go to the clubhouse 'til eight o'clock."

"Oh, I don't know what to think anymore!" Etta Mae said, yawning and rubbing her eyes. "I didn't realize it was so darn early."

"It's a mystery to me how you're even awake, especially after last night. What's going on with you anyways?"

Donnie hadn't honestly expected an answer, and had gone on to inquire about a particular article of clothing.

"Have you seen my gray paisley golf shirt?"

He frantically began sorting through a pile of clothing lying in a chair.

"I know I left it here . . . I've looked everywhere for it."

"You and that darn shirt." Etta Mae blurted, not actually admitting to having seen it.

"I sure hope you haven't put it in the wash, you know I never wash my 'good luck charm' whenever I'm in a tournament."

"The whole county knows you never . . ."

"That's a big no, no."

Donnie hurriedly continued searching, but chose to ignore his wife's callous remark.

"All the 'luck' might be washed out of it."

"Honey, I was going to tell you about this vision I had."

Etta Mae's mind had long since dismissed the whereabouts of the missing shirt, her thoughts had returned once again to her dream.

"I'm glad you got some sleep, because no one else did . . . *mainly me.*"

He stopped and watched his wife closely.

"Who could sleep with you mumbling and moving around?"

"I was . . . and you say I was mumbling too?"

"Yes, and you were talking some mumbo jumbo, so I figured I'd might as well get up and get a head start on my day.

That is, if I can find my darn shirt! Etta Mae . . . honey, you sure you haven't seen it?"

His wife's curiosity was now piqued to new heights regarding her fitful sleep. She stared balefully at the distracted man and yanked hard on his arm.

"You say I was mumbling? What was I mumbling . . . do you remember, honey?"

"Let's see I pulled my shirt off in the dining room yesterday."

"Honey, are you listening? Did you hear what I just asked you?"

"I'm sorry, but what did you ask me?"

He turned his attention to his wife once again.

"Oh yeah, when you weren't snoring, you were mumbling something like; "Yes, Lord. Yes, Lord."

"What're you talking about? I don't snore!"

"No you don't snore. Calling hogs is more like it, and it was loud!"

"Donnie, stop it! I said I don't snore!" Etta Mae defiantly repeated. "Now you, on the other hand . . ."

"Well, call it what you want, but it was like we had a concert going on." Donnie snickered. "And you were out snoring me, because it even woke me up."

He continued to replay his wife's bed-time drama.

"And then you started singing, and I thought you were going to leap right off the bed."

"Shut up . . . you lying!" Etta Mae playfully exclaimed. "And I was singing too?"

She couldn't help but laugh and reached out to take her honey's hand.

"Honey . . . *what* was I singing? Go on, sing it for me."

Donnie wondered whether or not his wife was losing it. He resolved to humor her.

"*Ah-h, now Ett-aa.*" He reluctantly said. "Okay, darn! I shouldn't even have brought it up."

"Oh, would you do it already!"

"Okay, okay!"

Donnie prepared to mimic his wife's rendition in a voice that was none too pleasing to the ears.

"I believe it went something like . . . . Un mm . . . G-God is still on the *thr-one*!" They both snickered.

"Then you started waving your arms and wiggling your feet."

Donnie's demonstration was a bit over exaggerated, to say the least.

"About that time I had had enough, so I jumped up and was going to go into the other room, but I remembered Delilah was in there. So, I went into the office and laid on the futon."

"Sorry, babe . . . I didn't mean to disturb your precious sleep, but I do remember feeling as if I was floating." She spread her arms in demonstration.

"Oh, and my sister will be with us for a couple of days. I hope you don't mind."

"Na, I don't mind. Why would I mind?"

"Oh, I knew you didn't, honey, but just out of respect . . . So, check this out, my dream went something like this; I was in this field plowing!"

She bounced up and down on the bed in the afterglow of her supernatural occurrence.

"*You; plowing?*" Now that had to be a dream."

"Quit it honey and just listen. Can you *please* do that?"

The over exuberant dreamer cast a meaningful eye at the love of her life.

"Okay, I'm all ears."

"Good . . . now like I said, I was plowing in a field, but please don't ask me what field, 'cause I couldn't tell you.

But, get this . . . there wasn't a horse, or an oxen pulling the plow, but just me walking behind it."

"Now, how're you going to up and plow a field without a horse or ox to pull it?"

A staunch look from his wife quieted the unwanted questioning.

"Sorry, my bad, please, do continue."

"As I plowed, the hard earth was breaking up, and the soil turned into this rich black dirt; you know, like rich potting soil. It was the blackest dirt I'd ever seen."

"You said blacker than potting soil?" Donnie interjected once again. "Now that's some black, and some rich soil."

"*Honey!* Would you stop with the *interruptions*, please?"

"Again, I'm sorry, just trying to picture you behind a plow. Now that had to be . . ."

"Donnie Le-Roy Smith, I swear, if you don't quit interrupting me!"

"Okay, but finish already! My Lord!"

"Well . . . Then I looked up, and the sky was full of clouds. But get this; the clouds were in the form of angels!"

"Angels?"

"Angels!" She reiterated. "And they were not just any clouds, but they were altocumulus clouds!"

"How'd we get from dirt to angels?" Donnie asked in amusement. "And now look at 'ya . . . They were alto-cumulus clouds. Go on baby!"

"It was a dream, dunce! I swear, if you don't stop interrupting me . . ."

"Alright now, it does not call for all that." The beleaguered man slumped down onto a nearby chair.

"Sorry, baby . . . but you just keep . . . anyway; the angels were the kind you see on Valentine cards. You know, the little cherub looking ones.

And the sky was full of them, and when I looked over to my right, there was a cloudlike form sitting on a throne!"

"*What-chu-say!* Go ahead girl!" Donnie excitedly urged his wife. A cloudy figure was sitting on a cloudy throne!"

"You big dummy, I just meant everything was composed of clouds."

His enlivened interest in the matter pleased her.

"Now mind you, I didn't get a good look at the figure, because that's when I woke up. Darn it!"

Donnie reached over to feel his wife's forehead. Her dream must've been something out of this world for her to be this worked up.

It had undoubtedly taken a toll on her emotions. He reasoned. He had never known her to carry on in such a way. But all in all, he did believe her.

He knew his wife spent a lot of time reading the Bible. So why wouldn't God appear to her in a dream? The caring husband had only ribbed his 'wittle munchkin' for a little comedic annoyance.

He had often watched her pour over the Scriptures nearly every night of their married life; so much so that dinner would sometimes be a quick microwavable entree.

But who was complaining? Not him. After all she did put up with his golf fanaticism.

"And so . . . as the world turns."

With this thought in mind, Donnie resigned to return to the task at hand.

"Don . . . honey, I believe I saw 'El Shaddai' sitting on His throne."

"Wow!" Was all the perplexed man could muster.

"As a cloud, now imagine that honey."

It was still too much for even her to fathom. She fell back on the bed curled in a fetal position.

"Like Isaiah 6 says; "I saw the Lord high and lifted up."

She rolled on to her back, cupped her hands behind her head and stared at the ceiling, mentally replaying the image in her mind.

"I swear, the more I live with this woman the more she never ceases to amaze me."

Donnie shook his head in bewilderment. "I can deal with her associating everything under the sun to divine providence, but I don't think I'm ready for this."

He bent over and began sorting through the scattered clothing once again. Eventually, his search led him into the walk-in closet.

"Oh, this is killing me. Where is my damn shirt?" He said, a little too forcefully.

His profane outburst startled his reclining wife. She raised her head from the pillow, but remained quiet.

"Well, I guess I'll just have to break in another one."

An unrestrained groan could be heard coming from the bed.

"Umm, please no."

The thought of having to endure yet another 'token of luck,' was a bit disheartening.

Yet, she would indulge his only obsession over and over again if it made her man happy. Still, the urge to taunt him was too irresistible.

"No-oo, surely you don't mean that, not another one."

The frustrated golfer didn't bother to respond to the friendly slight, and abruptly left the room.

"Oh, now my feelings are hurt!" The slighted woman feigned a sorrowful demeanor. "O, boo-hoo."

"Etta Mae, what are you grumbling about? It's not as if you have to wash it or anything."

Donnie yelled from the hall.

"No, I don't have to wash it! I can't get the darn thing off ya long enough to wash it."

He poked his head back into the room.

"All I know is, when I wear that shirt, my game is really on."

"But babe, you should be able to find it by the smell alone."

"Oh, aren't we the funny one." Donnie said under his breath as he journeyed down the hall.

Etta Mae had hidden the shirt in the clothes hamper. She had plucked the smelly lucky charm up by the broom handle as it lay discarded on the dining room chair.

"Sorry, my friend, but your luck just ran out, because it's all going down the drain."

Chapter Three

The morning's commotion had awakened the Smith's house guest who had flown in unexpectedly from New York the day before. Dee, as she was referred to by her siblings, practiced agnosticism.

Her religious views totally rivaled that of Etta Mae and Cynthia, their youngest sister.

You couldn't exactly call her an atheist, because she had believed in God once.

Delilah Whitman sauntered into her sister's bedroom with her pink silk robe securely tied.

"Hey, Sis I have to tell you, I'm not used to getting up this early."

"Oh, you don't say."

"What was all the commotion about anyway?"

"Umph, apparently along with everything else, my sister must also be a light sleeper."

Etta Mae patted the space beside her on the bed.

"Who knew you two early birds got up with the chickens?"

Dee continued to display her irritation while she yarned, then stretched.

"Slamming doors, banging drawers . . . and what's with this darn shirt?"

"Well, excuse us for living in our home." Etta Mae exclaimed, now also irritated. "We didn't mean to disturb your beauty sleep."

Besides, Dee still hadn't explained to her satisfaction, the reason why she had arrived so unexpectedly. The elder sister got up from the bed.

"Well don't you go getting all snippy with me Miss Etta!" Dee countered. "I'm just trying to figure out what all the noise is about."

"Sorry, Sis."

Etta Mae felt a tad regretful and only offered an apology to stave off the inevitable argument.

"I'm not usually up this early myself on a Saturday morning."

"So, why are you up?"

Delilah's gaze followed her sister's retreat. Etta Mae pulled at the edge of the window shades and peered out into the morning. Her mind had once again returned to her vision.

"Earth to Etta, hel-lo." Delilah frantically snapped her fingers. "Hel-lo, I'm talking to you."

"Huh . . . ? Oh, I'm sorry; you asked . . . what did you ask again?"

"What are you doing up?"

"I'm on call nearly every day of the week, so everyone knows it's my only day to sleep in. And you know what my Sundays bring."

"Church. Say, are you coherent right now?"

"Mmm, well from what I can gather, I disturbed Donnie too much in bed last night . . . apparently."

Genuinely concerned, Dee got up, walked over and turned her sister to face her.

"Are you alright? You look a little pale. That is if a black woman can look pale."

"You two weren't knocking boots last night were you? If that's the case, I didn't hear any screaming."

She gave her sister a playful nudge. The concerned sibling was hoping to bring a little humor into the suddenly chilled room, but her humorous efforts only received a blank stare.

Etta Mae desperately wanted to oblige her sister's efforts of keeping the conversation light, but she simply was not feeling it.

"Oh, little sister you wouldn't understand."

"No? Try me; whatever it is, it appears to have you floored. You're not your old self."

"What is my old self? It's not as if you've been around enough to know . . ."

"I know, and I know I should do better."

"Yes, you should."

"Anyway . . . so I heard you tell Donnie you had a dream, or was it a nightmare?"

Her sister's troubling behavior was so unlike the 'Rock of Gibraltar' Dee knew her to be. Nothing could chisel away her sister's porcelain veneer coated emotions.

Delilah hadn't seen her eldest sister in such a state of wonderment since she had learned of Grams pending home going.

She retreated back to the bed, leaving Etta Mae to stare out the window. The memory of their beloved grandmother's departure came to the forefront of her mind.

It had been a cold, rainy day in December 1985. She and her siblings had all gathered around their grandmother's hospital bed with each of their minds absorbed in loving memories.

"Good bye, Grams, I love you." Delilah had whispered.

"Tell Mom and Pop hello for us." Cynthia had said pass the knot in her throat.

Grams had smiled and had sought Etta Mae's face out of the three girls. The dying matriarch had called her name with a barely audible voice.

"Et-Etta Mae?"

'Yes, Grams? I'm-we're here, we're all here." Etta Mae had said with choking tears. The three sisters had taken hold of the feeble hands.

"It's up to you now . . . Etta Ma-Mae." The dying woman had stammered. "I tried to do my best by each of you." She had coughed. "It's up to you now . . . take care of your sisters." A series of coughs had followed her labored words. "It's time for me to go. I-I am ready."

Afterwards, Grams had focused her eyes on the ceiling. She had smiled, and with one last breath had closed her eyes.

Torrential flood gates had opened up, as personal dams burst forth. The hospital room had been filled with sobs. They held and comforted each other for quite some time.

The unusually harsh North Carolina winter had been hazardous to their grandmother's fragile health. Her health had been spiraling downhill for quite some time.

She had attended a close friend's funeral in a cold rain and had ended up with bronchial pneumonia.

The pneumonia had taken a toll on her weak lungs and she hadn't possessed the stamina to pull through.

Dee thought back on the tales her grandmother would tell them of her life.

Beulah Eileen Collins was their paternal grandmother's name. She had been born in Cartersville, a small town in North Carolina that boasted of being a small college town.

One day her husband, Thaddeus, had assumed he was only suffering with a bad case of indigestion, and had died on his railroad job while inspecting tracks.

However, the cause of death was later diagnosed as complications of an enlarged heart.

Beulah had reared her only son, James Anthony Collins alone, while earning a living as a second grade teacher.

Greenbrier Elementary School sat at the far end of a one-way street, surrounded by homes that once sported green lawns and picket fences.

The small town of 30,000 was located near the white sands of the Neuse River, named after the Neusioks, an American Indian tribe.

Their grandmother had told the girls tales of how the river was prone to extremes in its flow carriage, and often escaped its banks during wet periods.

When it was reduced to a trickle in the dry season, the river could be forded on foot.

Their grandfather, she had said would often go fishing when the water was at its normal level.

Unemployment had run high. The upkeep of the homes in the town reflected the state of the economy at the time.

Many of the prominent blacks had left town to venture north to cities such as D.C., or Baltimore.

The less educated factory workers were left to supply the makeup of the neighborhood.

James, their father, affectionately known as 'Jimmie' had been a fragile child. He had been prone to wheezing and catching colds at the drop of a hat.

So Beulah, ever the doting mother would dress her delicate son in double layers in the winter.

A knitted white cap, mittens, galoshes and a little blue snow suit served as his protected armor. A blue and white scarf wrapped up to his nose completed the ensemble.

On wintry days little Jimmie would often resemble a well-dressed snow man. The attire was so cumbersome their father would barely be able to lower his arms.

As a result, Jimmie learned to answer to the name of 'Michelin Boy.'

He spent many days watching from the sideline, longing to join in the fun with the neighborhood boys.

After graduating from Dunn High School, James had gone on to attend the College of Cartersville.

Any thought of going away to school was clearly out of the question. Beulah was not about to allow her darling only child to get away from her unfaltering scrutiny.

Donna Elaine Griffith had come into the life of James Collins one rainy day while the two dodged a sudden downpour.

The Devereaux Carter Library was an ideal place to study as it remained opened at least twelve hours daily. Many a late night study sessions had taken place during semester finals.

Donna's favorite secluded table had been in the non-fiction section of the library. The library had served as a refuge.

Gretchen, her roommate, an excessive chatter box left Donna no recourse but to frequent the library. It was the only spot that afforded her the peace and quiet she longed for.

Donna would lovingly run her fingers along the many books, and then settle on a title that caught her interest. Gretchen's over exuberance nature had resulted in their mother being well read.

Jimmie had sat at the table in the corner, and had sneezed into his sleeve.

"Bless you." A familiar female voice had said from between the row of books.

He'd heard that voice before in his 2 p.m. English Comp class. It belonged to a beautiful olive skinned young woman who sat about three rows behind.

He could listen to it all day; her voice had a way of sending chills down his spine.

As fate would have it, that chance meeting on a rainy autumn afternoon, had been the beginning of a whirlwind romance that eventually led to their marriage.

Subsequently, three darling daughters had made their union complete.

Unfortunately, their parents had died tragically in a plane crash. It had been a devastating loss for them all. Their paternal grandmother had taken the three sisters in to her home.

James and Donna Collins had been fun and loving parents, who always spent quality time with their daughters.

James at first, had wished for a son, but after having his first daughter, he couldn't have loved the four ladies in his life more.

Etta Mae, being the oldest of the three sisters had taken to mothering her two younger sisters with zeal after the loss of their loving parents.

Dee, the middle child, had resorted to finding outlets to cope with her grief.

She had tried finding solace in the homes of girlfriends by imagining she was part of a real family.

The youngest of the three girls was Cynthia, a silent shadow of a daughter, with a quiet demeanor.

Of the three sisters, Cynthia looked most like their mother; olive skin with a narrow nose set on a chiseled face with prominent cheek bones and hooded eyelids. Her shoulder length hair was often worn flipped at the ends.

Growing up, Cynthia had focused her full attention on finding the answer to the age old question.

"Why would a God who was all loving allow such a bad thing to happen to such 'good people' as her Mom and Dad?"

She would ask her grandmother and anyone else she thought would know the answer.

Etta Mae used to say she could only hope Cynthia's answer would be found in her Doctorate of Theological studies.

The recapture of Dee's cherished childhood memories are abruptly halted as Etta Mae turned from the window.

On second thought, she had decided to share the morning's escapade with her sibling.

"Sister, you're not going to believe this, but I had the most amazing vision this morning."

"You did?"

"You do know God is not limited to how He speaks, don't you?"

The look of skepticism on her sister's face did little to dispel her enthusiasm.

"I believe it was a vision, or maybe I was just dreaming, who can say. I may have been awake during it all. You never know."

"No, I wouldn't know." Dee sarcastically stated. "I haven't spoken to Him, and He certainly hasn't said a thing to me!"

She was overcome with frustration. The air of lightheartedness was dampened by the discussion of religion.

Etta Mae felt hurt, and looked at her sister with disbelief. The passing of time it seemed hadn't erased the gravity of her wayward sister's denial of The Creator.

"Well, I'm just glad He speaks to me. I don't know how you can live without Him."

She asked her sister an emotionally charged question.

"Exactly, how do you cope?"

"Oh, I manage just nicely thank you."

Now that the torrent of emotion had been released, there was no holding back.

"I believe you and Cynthia have enough religion for the three of us. You two live eat and breathe God.

Hallelujah this and *hallelujah* that. You can't even carry on a decent conversation without hearing "God said, or God revealed."

Etta Mae knew it would be fruitless to interact with her sister in this frame of mind, so she only listened.

"What had happened to the sweet little girl who once gripped Grams hand so tightly in church that in order to clap she would have to pry the little fingers loose?"

"She had believed once, so she's bound to believe again." Etta Mae thought.

Finally, she resolved to return to the topic of her dream.

"I wonder what He was saying, though. Cynthia should be able to tell me, so I'm going to call her today."

Dee decided to take advantage of her brother-in-law's entrance.

"Brother-n-law, is your wife always like this in the morning? Then if that's the case, I surely feel sorry for you."

Donnie looked at the sisters with amusement; he smiled and patted his wife's head.

"Have you heard about her angels?"

"My baby got the hook up to heaven!" He jovially shouted.

"Dee . . . I wish you could've heard her last night. I know she was asleep, but it was as if she was out of this world!"

"Say what?" Dee, playing the devil's advocate inquired in anticipation.

"What was she saying, or how was she acting?"

"Something like "Yes, Lord, praise God!" And get this."

Donnie responded with acute animation after realizing he had everyone's full attention.

"And then she started speaking some gibberish." He wiped the sweat from his forehead. "It scared the heck out of me."

Etta Mae looked on as the two are caught up in their comedic banter at her expense.

"Ooo! I bet you were about to crap your pants!" Dee added.

"Heck, ye-ah! I jumped up so fast and looked at her."

He continued his charade while his sister-in-law was overcome with laughter.

"And then she started waving her hands and singing."

He went even further to add how he thought his love may have become possessed.

"I'm just glad I made it out alive, heck, I thought her head was fixing to spin around and spit out green slime!"

"Donnie, you're crazy; and you say she was singing?"

Dee was overcome with uncontrollable laughter as she hung on to the wanna be stand-up comic's every word.

"So you got yourself a midnight serenade, I bet that freaked you out."

"Yep, you heard me. My girl was sing-ing. So I said ... what 'da hell?"

The two slapped each other a high five, but actually, the caring husband was truly concerned. He had found the night's happenings a bit unnerving.

"And check this out. This morning she believes she saw God *Almighty*."

"Oh man . . . now that's deep." Dee used the back of her hand to wipe away tears of laughter.

Donnie was only being amusing for his sister-in-law's sake. He had often witnessed his wife being caught up in the spirit.

God is so very real to him too. He also studied the Word, but in his own way and in his own time.

His wife doesn't know the extent of his knowledge. She naturally assumed the game of golf was more important to him than his faith.

"Hey, Bro-law, if you had stayed in bed long enough perhaps some of that holiness would've rubbed off on you."

Donnie stole a quick glance at his silent wife in time to see a hurtful look come over her face. Finally, he contended, enough was enough, so he decided to drop the fiasco.

He gave his wife a quick hug of reassurance, but Dee kept the jovial banter going.

"So that's why you decided to go golfing, aye?"

She gave him a slight punch on the shoulder with her fist.

"And what's up with this shirt you've been looking for high and low?"

The mention of the sacred icon was disquieting to Etta Mae, and a feeling of foreboding showed on her face.

The instigating sibling saw it as an opportunity to get a rise from her sister. She looked pointedly at Etta Mae and went on to ask Donnie.

"Do you really believe it's a good luck charm, or did you just have 'wifey' here lay anointed hands on it?"

Dee continued on to say. "I have to tell you, I'm finding you two to be some real characters."

"We're characters?"

Etta Mae was miffed and hurt by the dialogue in the room and decided to put a stop to it.

"So, if you two are finished!" She said a little too sarcastically. "I would like to say, I know I'm not crazy so you two can laugh all you want, but my *Daddy* doesn't show Himself to just any and everybody!"

"Ah . . . babe, no one is thinking you're losing it; huh Dee?"

Donnie gave his partner-in-crime a sly wink, but she simply smirked and looked down at the floor.

"Honey, Dee didn't mean what she said, or the way she said it for that matter."

He glanced at his suddenly quiet co-conspirator for confirmation.

"At least I hope she didn't." He questionably added

But his sister-in-law did little in the line of reassurance so he added yet another explanation.

"We just thought it all to be a little strange, that's all."

"Donnie LeRoy! I can't believe you! You of all people should know me by now. You know when it comes to the Gospel, I don't play!"

Donnie sensed the seriousness in his wife's voice and tried his hand at apologizing. He grabbed his love around her waist and pulled her close. He kissed her on the forehead and pressed her face into his chest.

"Oh honey, I'm sorry you felt I wasn't taking you serious."

The repenting husband pressed his lips to his wife's head and warmly muttered.

"Forgive me for acting a fool. And yes, I can see this means a lot to you."

Dee watched the two with indifference, but did not bother to offer any show of compassion.

"If you two could just have a Jesus encounter . . . just once!"

Etta Mae shouted as she tearfully pulled away from her repenting spouse. Donnie's arms dropped to his side in defeat. He shrugged his shoulders in bewilderment.

"Well, I don't know about y'all, but I think I hear a 9-iron calling my name. So I'm going to take my leave . . . ladies."

He leaned over to kiss his still perturbed wife once again before leaving the room.

"You two ladies have a nice day."

Etta Mae watched him leave with his don't-sweat-the-small stuff attitude. She secretly wished he would become more adamant in his faith walk.

She reflected on how he occasionally would attend Bible study at Shiloh Baptist Church that was held on Wednesday nights. When he did, he would sit quietly with his opened Bible, hopefully absorbing the lesson.

The concerned wife had no doubt her husband was a true believer, much unlike her sister, of whom she hadn't fully given up hope.

"Do you know what Dee?"

"Don't say it, because you know I don't want to hear it."

Highly annoyed, the agitated woman got up from the bed and left the room in a huff.

"Oh well, not to worry." Etta Mae concluded. "Today is a new day."

The slighted sibling clarified it by shouting out loud. "This is the day that the Lord has made, and I *will* rejoice, and I *will* be glad in it!"

With this self declaration, she climbed back into her California King bed, snuggled under the covers, and fell fast asleep; blessedly assured in her soul salvation.

Meanwhile, the rush of adrenalin began as soon as Donnie lifted his new stand-alone golf bag, and gently placed it in the trunk of his car. As always, he highly anticipated the start of a new game of golf. The new bag was filled with his old familiar clubs and irons.

The bag was the top of the line and was most ideal for the golfer going for a stylish look.

The bag's feature of a 6-Way top was the deciding factor. It boasted of having five-pockets with a water bottle sleeve, and the Pivot dual shoulder strap, which made it more comfortable to carry.

He hadn't wanted to replace his favorite driving iron, or the well-worn clubs. Their familiarity was too much to his liking.

His day was set. Other than the fact of missing his lucky icon, he felt equipped to do a little damage.

He made his way around the new Audi sedan he had purchased two months earlier for his wife. The pewter gray four door sedan remained stationary for the most part, unless she was going to church, or shopping.

It wasn't that his wife hadn't been appreciative of the generous gift, but for everyday use, she had preferred driving her old dark green Toyota Camry.

Donnie chalked it up to her simply having an only-use-the-best china-for-special occasions syndrome.

Saturdays were reserved for cleaning chores. It was also the best day to chat with her 'bestie' and next door neighbor, Tonika Gibbons.

He had to chuckle when he had once overheard them discussing the price of gas.

"Gir-rl did you see the price of gas has gone to $4.95 a gallon?" Etta Mae had asked. "It just doesn't make any sense."

However, Tonika's mind had been far from the price of gas. She had already supposed early on the crucial oil spill had driven the price of gas sky high. So to her the high gas prices hadn't been too surprising.

"Good, then maybe my significant other's pockets are lighter after filling up that pimped out ride of his."

She'd recalled how Josh had filled his gas guzzler up on Wednesday, but hadn't complained one bit about the astronomical price of the golden liquid.

"Oh, well." Etta Mae had simply said.

Donnie had noticed his neighbor hadn't said "my better half, nor had she made reference to my husband in the conversation."

Tonika hadn't been ready to discuss her problems at home, so she knew she had better add clarity to her off the wall comment.

"Josh just loves that ride of his . . . I think sometimes more than me."

Donnie thought about how he'd seen a pained look come across her face.

"Anyhow, I'm thinking about parking my old ride and footing it, or catching the bus to where I need to go." Tonika had added.

"Now, that's a joke." Donnie had thought to himself. "Not as long as my wife was around. He knew her friend wouldn't need to foot it to the curb." He smiled at the thought of their closeness.

Donnie dearly enjoyed ribbing his neighbor. In spite of it all she had a keen sense of humor.

But the one thing that could undoubtedly antagonize his friend to no end was to screw up her name.

"Sharmika, Chiquita, and especially, Tomika, were just a few of the mispronunciation he'd jokingly use.

Needless to say, her temper would spike to the utmost, which would amuse him to no end.

Life hadn't been too kind to his neighbor. When he and his wife had first met her, her first husband Jamal, a tall, robust, athletic, figure of a man had left her and an infant son high and dry.

Donnie was pleased his wife spent time with Tonika and wouldn't be surprised to hear of her complete conversion any day now.

"Shucks, if my saucy sister-in-law would stick around long enough, I'm almost certain her faithless stance on Christianity would soon be null and void."

Many thoughts filled Donnie's mind as he backed his black Buick out of the driveway.

He casually glanced over his shoulder in time to see Josh putting a suitcase in the trunk of his car. His wife could be seen through the front window wiping tears away.

"O, no! Don't tell me this one is on the run too? Damn! What's with that woman that she can't keep her man?"

Donnie honked his horn, and waved to the fleeing spouse. However, the friendly gesture was not returned. Donnie drove off puzzled by it all.

"Looks like my wife's shoulder will be soaked today with her friend's salty tears." He thought.

As he drove along, Donnie wondered how things would go with his sister-in-law being in the house. Her attitude this morning hadn't been the most pleasant he'd seen.

"No doubt my kind hearted, love of my life is sure to have her hands full." He said in the space of the car.

But he also knew his wife to be a mighty fortress. Any and all advice she would give either of them would be divine wisdom no question about it.

He thought how his wife had done a marvelous job rearing their only daughter, Dr. Janet Beulah Singleton, a clinical psychologist.

Janet lived in Hawaii with her husband Geoffrey, a general practitioner. From the looks of it no grandkids were on the horizon, but he could only hope there soon would be.

His wife, on the other hand, had simply resolved never to pressure the young couple in their decision making.

"It's their decision alone to make." She would duly note.

"Yep, my wife can handle it all, but as for me, the velvet green awaits."

"If I hit it right, it's a slice, if I hit left, it's a hook. If I hit it straight . . . then it's a miracle!"

"Mr. Woods eat your heart out!" He yelled into the air.

The hard-core golfer pressed his right foot a little harder on the pedal, sending the smooth ride slicing through the morning air.

Chapter Four

The beige suede couch still held Josh's imprint from where he had slept the night before. He had later returned after an abrupt departure. Neither he nor his broken-hearted spouse had sought the other out.

Tonika had heard him rise very early. He had retrieved the clothes from the floor where she had angrily thrown them after emptying drawers, and yanking clothes off their hangers.

"Get out you bastard!" she had screamed. "I don't ever want to see your cheating face around here ever again!"

Closet doors slammed shut, drawers opened and closed as Josh had gone about collecting his belongings.

He had reluctantly entered the bedroom to retrieve other personal items. She had sat on their bed and silently watched.

"I'll come back for the rest of my stuff when I find a place."

Tonika had followed him into the living room without saying a word.

She had stood at the window with tears streaming down her face, and watched as the candy-apple red, standard 10th Anniversary Trans Am sped away with tires squealing.

She had also watched as her neighbor backed his all too familiar black sedan out onto the street.

The puzzled look on his face hadn't gone unnoticed after having been slighted by Josh. There had definitely been a look of concern on his usually jovial face.

All in all, Tonika loved being married. She loved the thought of coming home to a traditional family; a home with a husband and …that all too important 1.1 child.

"What was that scripture again?" She pondered. "Oh I know. "When a man findeth a wife, he findeth a good thing."

"Josh had certainly found a good thang when he found me, because I certainly am a good thang." Tonika mused.

She couldn't help but to chuckle at her own Ebonic slang as she made her way into the kitchen. She looked around the disheveled room with indifference.

Dirty dishes had been left about from the day before. Even a jar of mayonnaise had been left open on the kitchen counter.

She hadn't had the strength to even care about housecleaning after experiencing the previous night's heart-wrenching torture.

"What life factors had driven the men in her life away?"

With Jamal she knew and could somehow understand. He had become overshadowed with a terrible state of depression after suffering their tragic loss. But with Josh . . . there was no excuse. She concluded. Hot tears erupted and flowed down her face once again.

"Mom, can I . . . may I have a bowl of frosted cereal?"

Ten-year old Ashad rubbed his growling belly as he ventured into the kitchen.

"Mom! Are you okay?"

The young boy rushed over to his mother and grasped her arm

to turn her towards him. Before she turned around Tonika managed to put on her best happy face.

When she faced her gangly, curly haired son, the mindful mother couldn't help but notice how much shorter her son's blue flannel 'pj's she'd recently purchased, now rose above his slender ankles.

"Oh, hey baby, surely, you can have as much cereal as you like. Here, let me get it down for you."

She retrieved the cereal from the overhead cupboard and poured her rambunctious son a hefty bowl of his favorite breakfast. She sat the box down in front of him, clearly knowing that one bowl would never be enough.

A warm motherly glow descended from the top of her head down to the tips of her toes.

The doting mother's chest swelled with pride at the thought of having reared such a handsome, well-mannered child.

Ashad was the spitting image of his Samoan father. She watched each day as little traits of Jamal emerged in her son. The way his ears moved when a broad smile swept across his face.

Tonika would lovingly pull at the dancing ears, which often resulted in much mother-son bonding. She turned to cradle his infantile face in both hands, hoping to plant a quick peck onto his cheek.

"*Mein liebschen! Ich liebe dich!*"

She uttered in her German mother's native tongue. Ashad squirmed and ducked his head to avoid the motherly smothering.

"Love you too, Mommy." He said, after he finally allowed her kisses to land.

She headed into the living room, afterwards. Yesterday's mail lay on the coffee table where she'd plopped it down.

As she sorted through the junk mail and the never ending bills,

Tonika's heart pumped wildly as she held an envelope from her doctor.

She'd gone for her annual check-up and mammogram last week. Diabetes tended to run in her immediate family, so he'd extracted blood samples.

"Oh, this must be the results of my blood test. I sure pray I don't have diabetes."

Tonika slid her index finger under the envelope's flap. Her eyes widened as she read the words on the page.

Your CD4 T cell count currently stands at . . . Tonika fainted.

Chapter Five

Etta Mae had slept for more than three hours. Finally, she awakened. Stretching in bed, she rose slowly and tied her favorite blue chenille robe loosely around her waist.

The backless navy velour house shoes made a slap, slap, slap, as she crossed the wood floor and made her way down the hall to the kitchen.

"*Blessed assurance, Jesus is mine, oh what a foretaste of glory divine . . .* O' my!" She said aloud. "Now that song is stuck in my head. Sister Brown must surely be wearing off on me."

"But, *praise the Lord anyhow!* It's a darn good feeling to know that He's *mine,* and I'm truly *His.* Amen!"

Her steps quickened as her nose followed the aroma of the morning's freshly brewed coffee, thanks to her thoughtful husband.

She poured a cup of the aromatic brew and settled down at the granite kitchen counter.

The hot liquid was all she could handle substance-wise; thanks to a nervous stomach. She looked around the well-kept home, pleased with her handiwork.

The coordinating shades of ivory and mocha color scheme greatly enhanced the décor of the adjoining rooms. Etta Mae loved her life and her home.

The Smiths called Chauncey, New Jersey, home. The neighborhood was a makeup of tri-level and ranch style homes lined on forested streets.

Staunch oak and sycamore trees dating back to the Pre-Civil War era, stood as if watchful guardians over each dwelling.

The houses varied in strict color patterns of taupe, kelly-green, brown, or muted gold set by the neighborhood association.

Jeremiah Joyner was the only resident who'd dared to challenge the rule, by painting his brown tri-level a bright lemon yellow. Needless to say, the hideous color was a major eye sore.

However, the defiant home owner soon came in line after being brought around by the stiff penalty he had incurred.

The Smiths lived in a 1,900 square foot, taupe three-bedroom ranch-home. Dresden blue shutters framed the casement windows. French doors led out to a two tiered deck.

She casually scanned the "L" shaped living/dining rooms from where she sat. The contented homemaker made a mental note to put her dust buster and vacuum cleaner to good use sometime soon.

Drying dishes left in a rack was the domestic vigilante's number one pet peeve. Thankfully, there were none to be seen.

The front and back yards was the priest of the household's pride and joy. The back yard's well-manicured sloped lawn was enclosed by a shellacked four foot high wooden fence.

A myriad of small, colorful fish swam nonchalantly in a bubbling man-made pond that was surrounded by an array of colorful blossoms. Donnie would lovingly tend to his horticultural masterpiece on Saturdays after a morning spent at the range.

Etta Mae moved to the solid mahogany dining table after

retrieving her Bible from the credenza. She had wanted to complete the final chapter of the Gospel of John for some time now.

Jesus' many spoken words and presence throughout the entire book was extremely inspiring, to say the least.

But, for some reason or other she just wasn't able to concentrate. For one thing her sister's troubling attitude continued to plague her thoughts.

Etta Mae inadvertently turned to a book other than John's. Her eyes fell on Hebrews, Chapter 12.

"Hum mm, now would you look at that? It says here," *Therefore, we are surrounded by such a great cloud of witnesses . . ."*

"Now, how co-incidental is that? First, I dream of clouds as to what I thought to be angels, and here I turn to this scripture. Hum mm . . . cloud of witnesses . . . hum mm."

"I just wonder if some of those witnesses weren't Peter, or Paul, or Mary." Etta Mae laughed at her own pun.

"Peter, Paul and Mary!"

Then another thought registered.

"Say . . . what if Mommy, Daddy and my dear, dear grandmother were among those clouds?"

The once joyous demeanor was soon overshadowed with solemn memories.

"Thanks for watching out guys! And Grams, I'm trying to keep all my promises I made to you . . . I'm trying with all my heart."

A lone tear trickled down her saddened face. The forlorn daughter sat deep in thought.

Sad thoughts continued to run through her mind. While she sat reminiscing, she had inadvertently chewed the top of her pen to a pulp.

Etta Mae grabbed a tissue to wipe the ink smudge from her lip.

The high level of stress she found herself in had begun to take its toll.

About that time her well-rested sister entered the kitchen wearing a bright floral, silk lounge ensemble. Etta Mae knew the ensemble could've cost as much as her monthly car notes.

The sound of her black high heeled mules topped with a puff of black fur was muffed on the crème Berber carpet. The elite socialite was always meticulous in her attire.

The shoulder length mane was swept up into a stylish French roll. Full lips as moist as a rose touched with a hint of morning dew sparkled from the red lip gloss she'd painstakingly applied.

She picked up a magazine from the coffee table. Dee cast a quick glance over at her sister, wondering if Etta Mae felt any better than she had earlier. She wanted to ease the tension that was so evident. Dee decided to draw her subdued sister into a conversation.

"Hey, Sissy . . . what are you reading?"

Etta Mae held up her Bible without bothering to look up, or to speak.

"Oh, I should've known it was the Good Book. I don't know why I even asked?"

"Well, why did you? I wouldn't want to surprise you or anything. You know what I mean?"

Yes, Dee knew what she meant. She'd seen and heard it all before.

"You remind me so much of Grams." Dee said. "Out of us three girls, she definitely rubbed off on you."

"Yep, you got that right. I listened, where as you . . . ."

Etta Mae does not finish the sentence. She hadn't cared to rehash the morning's discussion.

"Yeah, yeah." Dee merely waved her hand to dismiss the remark.

"And I know what you're about to say. And I'm about to say this. I'll give my life to *your* Jesus, maybe . . . like *tomorrow*."

She nonchalantly continued to flip through the magazine, when an interesting article caught her attention.

"Now would you look at this." She casually said. "Hear ye, hear ye, straight from the headlines! Preacher has reached a settlement!"

Etta Mae focused more intently on the scriptures before her. She'd read the magazine article last week, and had thought at the time, how it had probably made being able to witness to the lost more detrimental.

Needless to say, her sister's condescending attitude had proven that same fact to be true.

"It seems he'd been enticing young women with fancy cars and gaudy jewelry for a little tete-a-tete!"

Etta Mae willed herself to stay composed. If her condescending sibling felt her agnostic views were justified by the devious actions of a few fallen clergy, then so be it.

However, it would benefit her to know that when *all* stand before the risen King, he or she will only give account for his, or her good or bad deeds and no one else's.

"*Ha, ha, ha!*" Dee had let out a hefty laugh.

"Apparently, they weren't having the private conversations as that ole trifling rat had claimed. It says here the women sued his old butt for making sexual advances toward them. *Ha, ha, ha!*"

"Now that's just great. That's all I needed was for the queen of 'I don't believe' to read that one darn article." Etta Mae thought to herself.

"I'm glad that article is bringing you so much joy, but I for one fail to see the humor in it." She said to her sister.

"That's not surprising; you wouldn't." Dee retorted.

Etta Mae braced herself for the old that's-the-reason-I-don't-go-to church, plus the old, nothing-but-a bunch-of-hypocrites speech.

As it was, the many revelers she had approached for the purpose of witnessing would often throw that same hellish declaration back at her.

Along with; "why should I come to church and give that old highfalutin preacher my hard earned money?"

Then they would often add; "Just so he can live like a king. Besides, you guys are doing the same thing in church as we're doing out here."

Pastor Grantham had preached about the value of self-control; one of the nine fruit of the Spirit a few weeks ago.

"The flesh or the carnal mind was restless and wanted control over our lives. It is deceptive and causes the people of God to fall prey to all kind of temptations.

Only the Spirit of God can give one the power to take charge over one's flesh." Pastor had gone on to say.

Etta Mae recalled thinking how close his sermon had paralleled with what was happening to the unfortunate soul mentioned in the article.

Her faultfinding sister devoured the article with fervor. Dee wasn't done digging her claws into Etta Mae's righteous stance.

This article could undoubtedly be the arsenal she needed to use in her defense. She thought.

"I know you follow all those mega guys, so I know you know the preacher they're talking about here."

"Oh no, here it comes." Etta Mae groaned within herself.

"This is the one with custom made suits, and drives around in that white Bentley down there in good ole Alabama."

"That's not saying much, that could be any of them. It would appear money has become the idol of the day . . . perhaps that's the reason behind this very scandal."

"True, true, but you know what?" Dee went on to say. She absently snapped her fingers.

"Oh, here it is, Reverend Travis Thornton, that's his name. And I know you know him, or you've heard of him."

"Uh huh, I know him." Etta Mae interjected in a low voice. "And that's really too bad."

She felt a tightening in her stomach. The fact that a scandal such as this even came about sickened her to the core.

"Chalk one up for the devil." Etta Mae offered no further comment as she didn't care to give credence to the article.

"Spare me; *please*. . . that's a man of God all right." Dee bellowed while still deeply engrossed in the article.

"So, as it turns out the *man* of the cloth is no better than the rest of the world's damn ball busters!"

Etta Mae's highlighter fell to the floor. Her tingling spider sense signaled there was more to her sister's outburst than the article.

"What did you say?" She asked. "Sistah-Girl, can I tell you that this book says's; *"To be in the world, but not of the world."*

"So I just try real hard to keep my *"mind on things above, and not beneath."* Now do you feel me?"

"Yes, O' holy one, I feel you." Dee mockingly extended her hands and bowed. "And I can see you're about to spread those glorious wings and depart this world. So I'll concede."

"Don't go getting cute with me, Missy. And let me tell you something!"

"Go ahead, preacher-woman, tell me!" Dee defiantly shouted.

"I'm secure in my walk with the Lord." Etta shouted back. *"But,* can you say that?"

"Oh, girl, please, enough with the sermons already. Okay?"

Etta Mae felt a little disappointed for having responded so strongly.

She knew that if Dee was to ever return to her faith, it wouldn't be by her sounding 'holier than thou.' So, she backed off a bit.

"*Okay*, but I was about to let you have it with both barrels blazing."

"Well thank you for mercy." Dee humorously said. Then she changed the subject to something different all together.

"Me and this woman were talking on the plane . . ."

"And just what were you two talking about?"

"Oh, nothing much, we just struck up a conversation about an article she was reading. The article mentioned how laws are being passed that's changing the sanctity of marriage."

"*Oh*? And did you tell that woman on the plane you're on husband number . . . let's see . . ." Etta Mae finger counted. "Seven!"

"No, I didn't! Now, why would I tell a complete stranger my business?

And it's not even seven, thank you very much." Dee shouted defensively. "And if it was what would be so wrong with that? At least I married them."

"Yeah, you married, and married, and married them. Child, if it wasn't seven, I know it has to be at least six."

"Think what you like, but I do have something to show for my troubles."

Dee flaunted the mountainous rock that adorned her left ring finger.

"Okay, okay, nice rock if I do say so myself."

Actually the enormous gem had caught Etta Mae's eye when she met her sister at the airport. She couldn't help but be impressed with its size.

"So, I see diamonds really are a girl's best friend."

"Remember you said it and not me." The socialite brazenly polished the rock on her silk top.

"Yes, and if I recall . . . most of your husbands were way older than you." Etta Mae stifled a laugh. "And from the looks of it, you didn't walk away from those old coots empty handed."

"Honey, you haven't even lied." Dee raised her hand high to admire the glistening bobble once again.

The banter between the two sisters had taken on a lighter air. Etta Mae was grateful and continued ribbing her sister.

"Yes, because you certainly couldn't have been after them for their looks."

"Well now, I wouldn't go so far as to say that. Even if they were a tad bit my senior.

Of course, looks are not everything you know, but girl . . . it sure does help!"

Hysterical laughter filled the room. It was a welcomed relief from the early morning's tension.

"I'm surprised at you. Grams never could get you to eat prunes." Etta Mae said after composing herself.

"You use to say with your face all wrinkled up, and waving them away; "No, I don't like them 'cause they're all wrinkly!"

Rowdy laughter exploded once again, followed by a long silence. Finally, Dee broke into Etta Mae's thoughts.

"Speaking of Grams, have you heard from our little sister? I figure she's like you; out saving the world."

"Oh, sure, Cyndi called me last week. She said she'd tried calling you, but hadn't been able to reach you."

"Dang it, I hate I missed her call." Dee said.

"I guess she was calling to tell you she was going out to visit Janet and Geoffrey for a week. Of course, she should be back home by now."

"That's wonderful. The poor thing probably needed to get away from the rat race for a while."

"I'm sure she enjoyed herself. And you can bet Janet would've made sure of that."

"Well, if that's the case, then I have to get out to Hawaii myself one of these days. Maybe that's where I should've gone before coming here."

Dee couldn't kid herself. She knew there was no better place to be at this stage in her life, than with her alternate mother; her big sissy, Etta Mae.

Though, for reasons unknown, she had been shunning their sisterly embrace.

"Perhaps, if I don't think about *the problem*, then I don't have to deal with *the problem* until I'm ready." She thought.

"I'm sure glad my baby girl found her a good one." Etta Mae said. "Those two are sure to grow old together."

"And how's my niece doing anyway?"

"They're doing just peachie, and thank you for asking."

Dee caught the hidden insinuation in her sister's voice. She knew she should do better with keeping contact with her relatives, but her hectic New York life wouldn't permit it. She made a mental note to remedy that in the near future.

"I'm telling you girl, older gentleman can be all that and then some.

And you're talking to someone who knows. Besides, Viagra is always on the bedside table."

"Viagra! Etta Mae asked in astonishment. "Girl, do you mean all your husbands needed that stuff?"

"*No . . .* I wouldn't say *all.*"

Dee's declaration presented another opportunity to speak on the Bible. And Etta Mae took full advantage of it.

"You know . . . in biblical times, when God gave men the hook up, so to speak, I'm here to tell you, they were hooked up! Just ask Moses and Abraham!"

"Sister! You never cease to amaze me. I swear!" Dee shouted.

She merely shook her head as Etta Mae, not phased the least bit by her sister's reaction continued on.

"God restored their virility so they kept right on fathering children even after their bodies became prunes."

"Yes, I'm sure they did, but those women probably didn't have to look at their old puny butts either."

Dee said this to take the seriousness out of Etta Mae's comment.

The irony of her elder sibling constantly sneaking Bible lessons into their conversations annoyed her to the 'umph' degree.

"It's not like they romanced the women, or anything." Dee offered. "They, the women I mean, probably figured it was just their wifely duties. You see what I'm saying?"

For an instant, Etta Mae was speechless. She had never thought of it in that context. A shudder ran through her body just picturing the sexual exploits Dee's statement had conjured up.

"It's just like I said, you got to be pleasing to the ole' eyes to touch this!" Dee said, pointing to her womanly treasure.

"Oh! I'm sorry Dee, what were you saying?"

"Where's your mind now, weren't you listening? I was saying a man has to be pleasing to these eyes before he can . . . oh, never mind!"

"Girlfriend, that stuff's old school, because nowadays a woman takes her man at face value." Etta Mae said.

"And again, I say, it does help. Girl, you have to wake up to that image. And luckily none of mine wore dentures."

"So all seven of them had their own teeth, huh?" The elder sister inquired.

"All *thirty-two* of those mugs! Now I made darn sure of that."

Dee mockingly pulled at her own front teeth.

"And there you go with that darn seven again. Now I told you, it wasn't seven! It was *six*. And the last one, Damien, is much younger than any of them."

The two sisters are enjoying their easy chatter. Etta Mae recalled how short her sister's attention span was on settling down to one man, but like she said, at least she married them.

"So, what happened, the Viagra stopped working? Come on talk to me, Sistah-Girl."

"Etta Mae, stop it! You are so bad."

"I bet you thought you were safe with an old man, 'cause with the young handsome ones, more often than not; the more he's in love . . . it's with Emma, with Sue, and with Mary Jane.

Oh, and don't forget nowadays, with Tom, Dick, and just maybe Harry."

A pang of anguish hit Dee in the pit of her stomach. She rubbed the area while striving to keep a straight face.

"Alright now . . . I don't know about you but an ugly man can't do a thing for me!"

"Well, after seven husbands . . . ."

"Etta Mae! Now you're pissing me off. So stop it with the seven husband bull!"

"I'm just messing with you girl. Good grief! You talk about someone being touchy. Are you PMSing or something?"

"Yes I am, if that's what you want to call it. I appreciate your concern, but enough is enough. My goodness!"

Etta Mae sat in silence.

After much soul searching, Dee felt ready to open up. At least that would release all the built up tension.

After all, growing up, her big sister had been the rock she and Cynthia had leaned on throughout their childhood, and even into adulthood.

That thought alone had helped to bring about her decision. As painful as it was going to be, she felt she had to go through with the divorce.

"Shucks, it's because of a good looking man that I'm in this mess now. Biggest mistake I ever made in all my marriages."

"What was that baby?"

Etta Mae asked. She was elated the lid was finally off the box and speedily closed the space between them. She lovingly wrapped her hurting sister in a motherly embrace.

"Come here, baby girl . . . talk to me. How can Big Sis help?"

To her surprise, the once distraught woman pulled away.

Delilah had already concluded that divorce was her only option.

"I'm sure enough going to dance a jig when this one is over."

"So you are going through with another divorce?" Etta Mae inquired. "I just thought you were being your melodramatic self, as usual."

"Yes, I am. And I'm dead serious."

"Sister, are you sure about this?"

Dee firmly shook her head.

Etta Mae thought how she could tell when Dee stepped off the plane there was a major crisis brewing.

I'm just as sure as I am of being black and as you can see, I am black!"

"Well you're sure then, because you sure are.

"Oh, just stop it! I didn't know you were so bad." Dee said finding another laugh within her.

"Well you went there."

"Oh, by the way, thanks for putting up with me for a few days, until I get my bearings."

Dee pulled out a bejeweled compact from her pocket, and checked her flawless makeup.

Satisfied everything was in order she settled down to finish reading the magazine.

"You know you're welcome here anytime, honey. "Mi casa es su casa.""

Etta Mae reached over to pat her sister's hand.

Since Dee had opened the way for discussion, the opportunist decided she would dig a little deeper into the matter.

"Oh yeah, you never did say what the cause of all this was about. What did Damien do . . . or what did you do? You cast off men quicker than . . ."

"Quicker than what, Etta? You know . . . you just keep on pushing it!"

"I-I'm just concerned that's all. My word; again with the PMSing!"

"Well, just don't start with me again. I'll tell you what you want to hear, when I'm ready, but just don't push me!"

Etta Mae walked over to look out the window. The constant stressful dialog between the two was wearing her thin

"Ummph, that's strange, Josh's car is gone. Wonder where he and Tonika went."

"Don't get me wrong." Dee said from across the room.

"I knew he was a little too young, but Damien is a looker. That's probably what attracted me to him in the first place."

"Wait a minute! You say he was young?"

Etta Mae turned with a puzzled look on her face.

"You into making headline news now like those cradle robbing school teachers?"

"Ha, ha, aren't you funny? Let's just say, I've had them old and now I've had them young. So there, what's it to ya?"

"Oh, it's nothing to me, sister. Just as long as no cradles were robbed while you were having them young. You'll free to do whatever tickles your fancy."

"Well, thank you mother for your permission." Dee said, curtseying in jest.

"I should've known something was up with you. It's not as if we were invited to your quickie wedding."

"No time to waste. It was a whirlwind romance and before I knew it, I was Mrs. Damien Whitman."

"And just like that you became Mrs. Delilah Carol Collins Melvin Cox Jefferson Whitman.

Oh wait, I forgot one; Simmons! I can't leave him out." Etta Mae said breathlessly.

"Stop being so mean, would you!" Dee said in her defense. "I'm just doing what's done in society, especially by men, but no one talks about just how many times they marry. Now do they?"

"Now Delilah . . ." Etta Mae cautioned.

"Besides, I'm not the first, and I certainly won't be the last. What's good for the goose is certainly good for the gander!"

"No! That's not true . . . and I wouldn't go throwing any morals away, just because the world says it okay."

"Are you forever preaching? Geez!"

"No, but I'm just saying the ways of the world will have you going to hell with a coat on. After all, the world is the system of Satan you know."

Dee chuckled at her sister's sanctimonious view on life.

"Honey, let me tell you this one thing . . . Miss Delilah lives her life the way Miss De-li-lah designs to live it. And besides, I couldn't stand to part with my luxurious mink coat anyway. Say . . . you sure you won't join us heathens?"

"Delilah Carol! Now, don't you play with me like that!"

Etta Mae made a playful airy swipe with her hand in her sister's direction.

"I won't be in that basket with you bunch of . . ."

"Are you sure?"

"*Listen here*, when that sweet chariot swing low . . . honey; its surely going 'a let me ride, because, I surely got a home on the other side." Etta Mae definitely stated. She lifted her eyes and hands to heaven.

"Well, ride on King Jesus!" The defiant one playfully said.

"Be careful now you're on the verge of blasphemy."

"Sorry Sis. You're right, but even you know there're plenty of women who're looking to the fountain of youth when it comes to their men."

"Cougars, I believe they are calling them now." Etta Mae said in agreement.

"I know what they're called; I'm not that much out of it that I don't know the haps!"

"Well, you do think too much inside the box when it comes to life in general. But I suppose that comes from your upbringing!" Etta Mae said.

"And I know you've got to be careful out there, because the world is certainly different than it was when we were growing up. Of course, I could be wrong, so don't quote me on it."

"Oh, you don't have to worry about that, it's not something I care to repeat."

"I'm sure you wouldn't, but look 'a here, even in biblical times, they had to fend off ole slew foot. So why do you think today would be any different?"

"I never said it was." Dee said, preparing herself for another of her sister's biblical renditions. And Etta Mae didn't disappoint her.

"Girl, let me tell you. There was this woman in the scriptures that had seven demons . . . ."

"Okay, okay, stop right there. I don't want to hear anything about some possessed woman way back when."

"Now you see that's the problem. Do you think the Scriptures were written just to collect dust?"

"I don't know, but I'm sure you're about to tell me." Dee cupped her head in both hands and shouted.

"Please! Somebody . . . rescue me!"

Chapter Six

Just the thought of something like contracting the HIV virus was too farfetched for the relieved man. The counseling/testing center had been very adamant about the perils of practicing unsafe sex. He'd finally realized the danger he'd put himself in, not to mention his wife.

Damien Whitman was thankful mother luck had been on his side as his fingers closed around the apartment keys.

He had returned to the home he shared with his socialite wife, after a rough night alone at a nearby hotel. He had left after their ferocious confrontation. There certainly had been no reasoning with her at the time.

The lock clicked as he turned the key. The heavy metal door easily swung open after a forceful push. He entered not knowing what to expect.

He had hoped by now his wife was ready to discuss the issue in a more civilized manner.

The apartment was empty. Damien rushed into the luxurious gold and white embossed paneled bedroom. There, all he found were opened dresser drawers and closets, the evidence of hurried packing.

He stood in the center of the room and dropped to his knees. His body was racked with great gulping sobs.

Damien hadn't meant for his mere curiosity to go that far.

He'd meant to end the impromptu encounters months ago.

"Just this last time and no more, I swear." He had mentally promised himself.

The whole fiasco had all started with that one chance encounter on a rainy day.

Keith Easton a deceptively manly man, tall, dark and handsome had been an Account Executive on Wall Street.

Coincidentally, he and Damien had met while hailing a cab on a busy New York street.

Drenched in a down pour, they'd both reached for the cab's handle simultaneously. Damien was willing to forego his claim and offered to catch another one as so did Keith.

"Oh, I'm sorry this one is yours, I'll catch another." Damien had offered.

"No you take it." Keith had retorted.

A young lady standing a few feet away had watched the scenario being played out.

She had suddenly whisked past the two gentlemen; opened the car door; and had settled in the back seat and had directed the driver "Twenty-fifth and Broadway." And away the cab went.

The two perplexed gentlemen had been left standing in the rain.

They had sought refuge in a nearby bar while awaiting the end of the downpour, and had struck up a progressive conversation.

They had hoped to be able to savage what was left of their now possibly ruined Italian suits.

Formal introductions had been made. Likes and dislikes had been discussed.

Finally, marital status became the topic of interest. Keith it seemed had never married and had shared with Damien that he was gay. Strangely enough, Damien was taken aback by the well dressed bank executive's declaration.

He had coughed as his third vodka and martini had found its way down the wrong pipe.

Keith had reached over and had given his back a few whacks.

"You alright partner!"

Keith had allowed his hand to linger. He had begun a slow circular rub on Damien's back.

Their eyes had met. Keith had already sensed the questions forming in the nervous gaze that stared back at him.

He'd seen that look before; curious, but not bold enough to venture into unchartered terrain. His hand had kept up the steady motion.

The distraction of the constant rubbing had caused confusing thoughts in Damien's brain.

Confused by the unwelcomed feelings, he'd reached to remove the surprisingly soft, manicured hand only to have it covered instead by the conjurer's other hand.

"I-I'm okay, uh, hmm, sorry."

Damien had stammered as he took another gulp from his glass.

The stealthy conjurer had leaned in for a presumably long kiss. Damien had pulled back at first, and had lowered his head.

Keith, not one to be dissuaded by the man's shyness, had brought his face closer and the two had openly kissed.

They had talked long afterwards. Keith had emphasized that even married men were prone to walk on the wild side every once in awhile.

It was at that point that the two gentlemen had decided to take their mere encounter a little further.

Going out into the sunny evening they had arrived at Keith's swank apartment.

The tryst had ended almost as soon as it had begun. After getting to know Keith more intimately, Damien had decidedly found that he hadn't cared for the promiscuous lifestyle of his initiating partner.

But the one sure thing that had come out of the chance relationship was the homosexual tendencies that had once lain dormant in the man-on-man novice had now been awakened.

He had discreetly begun pursuing the newly discovered desires, all while carefully playing the role of a doting husband to an unsuspecting Delilah.

Damien Darnell Whitman began life as an only son in a small Georgia town as a preacher's kid.

He had grown up hearing the Word, night and day, day and night.

It would be hard pressed for anyone to understand what he'd endured and surprisingly enjoyed while growing up.

He vividly recalled the many late nights spent with his heavy head bobbing up and down with spittle drooling from his lips, straining to stay awake during his father's many late night services.

The 'Tabernacle of the Congregation Holiness Church' in a little town in Georgia hosted a small congregation made up of mostly matronly women.

Very few of his peers docked the burgundy carpeted sanctuary.

The wooden benches hadn't exactly been the soft padded cushions the well defined derrières sat on today.

His father's office had been situated inside the church's parsonage, located next door to the church.

Damien could often hear Pastor J.J. Whitman discussing private matters with his parishioners.

He had learned not to ask any questions about anything he'd overheard, or whose problems were being discussed.

The naive youngster had once made the mistake of inquiring, only to receive a serious paddling from his father who had insisted on his confidentiality.

The years had flown by and like the dutiful son he was, Damien had remained loyal to his parents and that little church.

If there was anything he could attribute the life style he now led would be the traumatic incident he once suffered in his childhood.

One day while he was alone cleaning the men's toilettes, a staunch male member of his father's congregation had forcibly raped him in a toilet stall when he was just thirteen years old.

Afterward, the violated lad had been threateningly warned never to divulge the incident to anyone, which he never did. He had silently relived the horror of that day for many years. Apparently, the perverse seed of homosexuality had thus been planted.

While in college, years later, both his parents had passed away. His father first and then a year later his mother.

After his mother's funeral Damien had never returned to the little church or to his hometown.

Fortunately, after attending a historically black college in Georgia, he had landed a job as a Hedge Fund Banker in the financial district of New York City.

The job afforded him a profitable life. A substantial savings account was the result of hard work.

Delilah, a popular recently divorced socialite, who frequented the inner financial circles of the high class society, soon came into his life. He knew her to be at least ten years his senior. The age difference had done little to daunt his interest in the designer clad vixen. Besides, in today's society, he had reasoned, age was nothing but a number.

Delilah had joined the ever growing number of older women who found dating younger men more pleasurable than dating men their own age or older.

The fiery courtship had begun and had eventually led to marriage.

Damien suppressed the thought that perhaps subconsciously, he had sought a mother figure more so than a wife in the May-December relationship.

The now distraught husband sat in the middle of the floor. His mind refocused on the plight he now faced.

Delilah had walked in on him and his latest conquest in her mahogany four poster bed.

Dumbfounded, she had let out a blood curdling scream.

Damien was so sure she would take the usual full four hours at her weekly 10:00 spa that he'd somehow gotten careless.

But a throbbing ingrown toe nail on her right foot had prompted an earlier than usual return home.

The effeminate young man had just been a pick-up at the same high-end bar he and Keith had met.

"How could you!" She had screamed, bursting into tears. "Damn it to hell! How could you!"

The agonizing look on her face would forever be branded in his memory.

"I have to go after her!" Damien decidedly declared.

The short flight to New Jersey would allow little time to think of what he would say or do, but still he forged ahead. The determined man grabbed his medium size Carrington luggage and threw in a few items of clothing and toiletries.

Damien's thoughts ran amuck as he rode down the elevator. The uncertainty of his future gave way to a sense of urgency.

He hailed a yellow cab and jumped into the backseat.

Delilah had shared many stories with him of her childhood.

He knew how much her big sister meant to his wife.

"To LaGuardia please! He shouted to the turban wearing Indian driver.

Damien made a phone call while en route to the airport.

Chapter Seven

Etta Mae poured herself another cup of hot coffee. She cast her eyes out the window and saw her neighbor dragging her trash to the curb.

"Mm mm, I wonder what's up, wonder why she's putting the trash out and not Josh."

She had not realized she had spoken aloud.

"Something's happening over there . . . and I still don't see Josh's car."

The defiant sibling felt guilty about her earlier harsh reply and came up behind Etta Mae fully intending to offer an apology.

The moment of bonding was stolen as her eyes followed her sister's gaze.

"Oh, I see your best bud is coming over . . . I'll be in my room."

"Yes, that's Tonika, you remember her, don't you?"

Dee gave Etta Mae's shoulder a reassuring touch, and retreated down the hall. The last thing she wanted was to be drawn into any gossip.

Tonika lightly tapped the doorbell before letting herself in. Etta Mae sat her cup down and the two friends exchanged hugs.

"Hey, neighbor! What're you up to on this fine Saturday morning?"

"Oh, about 5' 7" and a 130 lbs." The witty neighbor helped herself to a cup of coffee.

"I just took out the trash so I thought I'd stop over to see what was up with you."

She glanced around to make sure they were alone. Tonika hadn't wanted to share her marital woes in front of Etta Mae's sister.

"I see your old man has left for the green already."

"Now how'd you guess? He should be home in a little while, and what ya wanna bet, the first thing he's going to say is; what's for dinner?"

"He probably will at that. You know your hubby so well."

Etta Mae raised the cup to her lips, but lowered it, and decided instead to address the elephant in the room.

"Toni, why were you messing with the trash . . . where's Josh?"

Tonika's head slowly dropped as she sat in silence and stared into her cup. Words just could not seem to make their way past the lump forming in her throat.

"My sister Dee is here somewhere; if she comes out of her room, maybe you'll get a chance to meet her."

The understanding matron reached over and patted her hurting friend's arm.

"And girl, you know you don't need any excuse to come over here."

Tonika covered Etta Mae's hand with her own and squeezed it gently.

"Dee came in from New York yesterday?"

"Yep, I picked her up at the airport at exactly 12:20."

"Ooh, I see she's still a stickler for time. I remember when she was here last . . ."

"She may be, but it doesn't matter to me."

"Sounds like you weren't expecting her."

"I wasn't, but she's welcome anytime she wants to pop in. You never know with Miss Dee."

"It must be nice." Tonika said. "Everybody ain't got it like that."

"Ah girl, she's just going through something right now. I'm just glad I can be here for her."

"Do you know what she's going through?" Tonika asked, stirring sugar in her coffee. "Having problems with hubby maybe?"

"Couldn't tell you something I don't know. And if she knew I was discussing her *business* . . ."

"Miss Etta . . . you're always there for everyone . . . even me."

"Whoa, where did that come from . . . what's up Toni? You're acting like your world just ended."

Etta Mae gave her amigo's hand another reassuring squeeze.

"I'm here darling, I'm here." This time she grasped both hands.

"I just don't know what . . ."

Donnie came in from the garage at that moment with his golf clubs and left them to stand in the middle of the kitchen floor.

Tonika hurriedly wiped her face with her sleeve, and sipped her coffee.

"Whew! I'm glad to be out of all that humidity."

He soon realized he'd walked in at an inopportune moment after he noticed what looked like tears on his neighbor's face.

"Sorry for barging in, but it looks like you two had a pity party going on. Tonika, girl did your cat die or something?"

"Honey . . . now have a heart. I don't think your friend is up to your usual antics this morning."

Then Etta Mae turned her attention to the discarded golf bag.

"And are you going to leave that golf bag right there?"

"Ya think!"

Donnie opened the refrigerator and took out a cold beer.

"Sweetie, I know you're proud of your bag and all . . . and it is quite exquisite, but your boys don't belong in the middle of my kitchen."

"Yeah, yeah, I'll move 'em in a minute."

After taking a long swallow from the cold thirst quenching liquid, Donnie touched the cold bottle to his sweat moistened forehead.

"I just need to practice my putting skills. Why . . . are they bothering you or something? How's Ashad, Tomika?"

"He's doing fine, thanks for asking." She said in a barely audible voice. "The Johnsons are picking him up for practice in a few hours."

"Oh, that's good. So he plays soccer with Brenda and Hank's grandkids?"

"Yes, he and Jared are good friends."

"And the answer is no, to your question, honey." Etta Mae interjected.

"They're not bothering me, but still, I don't want to trip over them later. You know how forgetful you can be."

"I can see the old girl's not herself, but she'll bounce back in no time. Right, To-mi-ka?"

He gave his friend an old 'atta girl' nudge.

The concerned friend that he was, Donnie thought perhaps butchering her name would draw his saddened colleague out of her funk.

He wanted to create a much needed smile on her gloomy face.

"To-mi-ka, you drink all my coffee?"

Tonika realized that now wasn't a good time to bear her dirty laundry.

She composed herself and decided she may as well join in the friendly banter with her pesky neighbor.

"Donnie Leroy Smith! Would you get hooked on phonics? My name *is* . . . Tonika! With an 'n,' thank you very much."

"Tonika, Tomika, Chaquita, whatever!"

Donnie gave his wife a quick kiss on the cheek before taking another sip of beer.

"Lord, you sure are pouring it on a little strong." Tonika jokingly said to Donnie.

He responded to her remark by distorting his face.

"Anyway, baby . . . what's for dinner?"

"Hey, Sweet Daddy!" Etta Mae gave her friend a knowing wink.

"I'm glad you're back, I missed you this morning. Not unlike any *other* Saturday morning."

"I just bet you did." Donnie said, as he turned his attention to their neighbor once again. "To-*mi*-ka, your lights get cut off again, the reason you're here?"

"No they didn't because your wife took your grocery money and paid my bill. So there!"

"Now . . . honey!"

Now pleased with the reaction he had finally invoked from the once forlorn neighbor, Donnie took it a little further.

"Darn it, I know you didn't spend any of my hard earned money on old Miss Thang here.

Not when there're candles in the kitchen that ole Miss Down-On-Her-Luck could've had."

"Now honey you know I take better care of your money than that."

The ladies feet made contact under the counter.

"Um humph, I know your ole bleeding heart . . . everybody's a neighbor self." Donnie quipped.

"What money?"

Tonika asked while she pushed even harder against her friend's foot.

"You sure you didn't get your pink slip yesterday?"

"You're joking right?" Donnie asked.

"Well you're on that damn golf course too much for someone claiming to be working." Tonika added.

Laugher filled the cozy kitchen. Tonika felt much better, now that she was able to laugh.

"I know that's right." Etta Mae chimed in.

Despite her somber mood, Tonika felt obligated to keep the jovial banter going.

"With all those budget cuts going on . . . Etta, girl if I were you I'd call his job on Monday."

"Excuse you! I don't recall sleeping in your bed! And why are you so concerned about my job? Last time I checked my pay stub, it read Donnie L. Smith!"

"And . . . I believe I have a blessing on the way."

Tonika rubbed her thumb against her fingers and then pointed to Donnie. "And I'm looking at 'im!"

"Humph, Negro, please, you wish." Donnie slapped at Tonika's hand.

"My dear friend, now you're supposed to "love your neighbor as you love yourself." Tonika said. "That's Scripture, now am I right Etta?"

"Tonika baby, I'm no fool . . . I loves you, but we ain't exactly got it like that."

She grabbed her man around his waist.

"I just can't be wasting my Boo's hard earned cash."

"Ha! Now you talking baby. It's good to hear my money is in good hands!"

Donnie playfully pulled away from his wife's grasp and bent down to be eye level with his neighbor.

"And for your information Miss All-Up-In-My-Busi-ness. I just happened to have gotten a raise just this week. Thank you very much."

This time he directed his attention to his wife.

"Babe we're in the money! No budget cuts here, no sir-ee."

"O, Boo! Why didn't you tell me?"

His wife playfully whined. She grabbed her husband around his waist once again.

"Tonika, gir-rrl, we're going shopping."

"Oh, no you're not! Not on my money, you're not. That's exactly why I didn't tell your old butt in the first place!"

He unclasped his wife's hands and stepped away.

"I tell you, a man always has to keep an ace in the hole just to get ahead."

"But Hon-ey . . ." Etta Mae said with pouted lips. "You've been holding out on me. O' Boo, I'm crushed."

"Don't but honey me, a man has to draw the line somewhere, especially when it comes to his pockets."

The conversation is interrupted by the ringing of the phone. Donnie went over to answer it.

"Hello? Who is this? . . . Who?"

He turned and gave his wife a puzzled look.

"Yes, this is the Smith's residence . . . Is . . . excuse me! Who's gone? Now look here, before I answer any of your questions, I think you'd best answer mine. So, who may I say is calling?"

Donnie heard a click at the other end of the line.

"Damn! The fool hung up!"

"He hung up, was it Damien?" Etta Mae asked. "He didn't want to talk to his wife?"

"The fool didn't say who he was, and not like I know him from Adam."

Needless to say, Donnie was a little miffed over the whole conversation.

"Well, I can see he got under your collar." Etta Mae said.

"You're darn right! I sure wasn't about to give out any answers …unless he had given up some. Now would you?

This time he drank deep from the bottle in his hand.

"But still, you should've known who it was." Etta Mae said defensively. "No one else would be calling for her here. At least, I don't think."

"Who can keep up with the men in your sister's life?" Donnie blasted.

"It's not like we've ever met him. Although . . . I did hear him say, something about he didn't even know she was gone, before he abruptly hung up."

The phone call only made the fidgety mother-hen more anxious to get to the bottom of her sister's situation.

Tonika concluded the sorrows of her life would need to be put on hold. From the sound of it, a more pressing issue was at stake in this household.

Donnie fished a ball out of his pant pocket and grabbed a putting iron from the free-standing golf bag. One of Etta Mae's beige and blue floral patterned Pfalzgraff coffee mugs served as a makeshift receptacle.

"Whatever was going on between his sister-in-law and her husband was none of his business." He decided. Donnie tapped the ball and sent it scurrying.

But, true to form, all his calculated efforts proved futile as the ball bounced off the cup and rolled under a kitchen stool.

His second attempt was no better than the first. This time the ball didn't go anywhere near the cup but rolled under the dining table.

"What's your problem today?" He shouted to the misdirected ball.

"Well, Donnie." Tonika jokingly said. "That's no surprise; we can't exactly call you Mr. T. Woods now can we?"

Donnie turned his back to her taunting humor. As for Tonika, she had just gotten started and wouldn't let up.

"If you ask me, I'd say you're more like a Tigger." The women shared a laugh. "Now where did you abandon Winnie?"

"Woman, I don't know what you're talking about. I may not be the Tiger, but I am his big brotha!"

"You wish." Tonika countered. "Last I heard his momma only had one son."

The little white ball's refusal to go into the cup had Donnie's nerves on end. His concentration was off, thanks to his neighbor's constant chatter.

"And why should today be any different?" Tonika said, smirking. "Let's just say, the only green blazer you'll be wearing is the one you buy."

"Oh, Lord, I pray it's not a green one. He won't be going anywhere with me in a green blazer!" Etta Mae added, even though…the puzzling phone call continued to plague Etta Mae's thoughts.

"Forget you! Tonika."

Donnie had become increasingly agitated with the two women for doubting his golfing skills.

"It's not as if I'm trying to get a Ryder's Cup, damn it! Etta Mae you'd better get your girl; before I knock . . ."

"Before you do what?" Tonika jumped up with blazon fists. "And I suppose you haven't met Bert and Ernie here."

"*Ha, ha, ha!* Sit down girl. Now you two numbskulls behave."

Etta Mae playfully stood between the two warring parties and jokingly slapped her friend on the arm.

"Do I have to get my strap?"

"Your strap?" Tonika asked. "Oo! Etta Mae, you have a strap? It wouldn't be a two prong whip, now would it? Ooh, that's so kinky!" She found her friend's threat a bit humorous. "You two old coots."

"Uh, slow your road Miss Freak-a-zoid." Etta Mae interjected. "And get your mind out of the gut-ter. We ain't down like that. Huh Boo?"

Donnie was oblivious to the garish humor.

"Nope, the Tiger don't have to worry about me taking any of his trophies."

Then in mid thought he turned his attention back to the women.

"Say, didn't I ask about dinner earlier?

"Yes, you did, I can attest to that." Tonika said.

"Thanks, friend." Etta Mae chided.

"Well, what're we having, wife of mine?"

"Yes wifey. What exactly are we having?" Tonika mimicked.

"*We?* Since when do we include Donnie, Etta Mae and To-mika?" Donnie jokingly blasted.

"You won't be parking those size tens under my table tonight." He added.

They all laughed.

"Surprise yourself, honey, and make me and my friend here dinner too while you're at it."

"Yes Tiggy, a nice juicy steak would go good right about now.

And I want mine raa-re." Tonika mimicked a tiger's roar. "*Roa-aaaar!*"

"Here Cha-mi-ka." Donnie made a fist. "I got your rare steak alright, but it won't be as rare as your lip."

Tonika returned the gesture, before getting up to get a drink of water.

Donnie sent a blaze of light hearted questions her way.

"Is your husband working yet?

And what kind of work does he do? Where is he anyway? Shouldn't you be with him?"

"Now, be nice, honey!"

Etta Mae quickly intervened, in an attempt to salvage her bosom buddy's emotions. She understood her unsuspecting companion was up to his jovial antics once again.

"*An-nd* . . . once again butthead! My name is To-ni-ka! And my husband is an entrepreneur. He's just in between projects at the moment. Thank you very much."

Oh, so now Josh's job is . . . ." Donnie imitated washing a phantom windshield. "Hello sir, mind if I wash your windshield? Ah, that'll be two dollars, please."

He jumped backwards from the imaginary car and yelled. "Hey! Watch the toes!"

"Honey you're so bad. Please leave Tonisha alone. Oops! I meant Tonika. Sorry, friend."

The husband and wife slapped hi-fives.

The benignant neighbor couldn't help but laugh despite herself. This was the reason she so enjoyed coming over to visit her friends.

If you were ever in a funky mood, it wouldn't last long around these two.

"Tonika, girl don't pay that class clown any mind, he's just being silly."

"Him . . . what about you? You're getting just as bad, but you know what? You two numbskulls are not going to worry me."

The house guest defiantly crossed her legs, and turned sideways in her seat.

"That's good, because you know we're just jiving." Etta Mae said. "Besides girl, we women have our ways when it comes to men anyway. Don't we?"

"At least some of us seem to." Tonika said distractedly.

"Oh my, I wasn't expecting that remark. I must say, you're acting a bit strange today." Etta Mae said with concern in her voice. "There wouldn't be anything specifically you wanted to tell me, would there?"

Tonika looked from Donnie then back to Etta Mae. She finally decided to lay her soul bare.

"O' what the heck." She finally said. "I'm sure you've already figured it out by now. Josh is gone."

"Oh, no! So that's it! I was beginning to wonder." Etta Mae exclaimed.

Yep, I'm afraid so. He left yesterday, then returned late last night and slept on the couch."

The distraught woman's tears flowed freely once again. Etta Mae went over to where she sat and gave her a tight squeeze.

"Where'd he go?" She asked.

"That, I couldn't tell you. All I know is he left again this morning after packing most of his belongings."

"So, that's what he was doing when I saw him?" Donnie said, as he watched the scene before him. He went over to the two women.

"You mean my boy Josh has flown the coop? Like out of here? See ya! . . . I can't believe it!"

"Oh, stop with the questions already!" Tonika said, with bullets for eyes. She was not the least bit amused.

"Just let it go, I don't want to talk about it!"

"Tonika, girl, you have my permission to slap him!" Etta Mae said.

"And it's okay if you don't want to talk about it. I totally understand."

Etta Mae became irritated at her husband's lack of sensitivity. She silently mouthed for him to keep quiet.

"Thanks, I really appreciate you. And there's nothing funny about it, broomstick!" Tonika kicked at the snickering menace.

"Sure ain't." Donnie said. "Not in the least bit, imagine that. No wonder the dude . . ."

"Oh, would you just please let it go already!" Tonika shouted.

"Uh-oh, it's getting hot in here." Donnie wittingly said. He wiped his forehead with the back of his hand.

"Oh, but for God sake, don't take off any of your clothes."

His whole determination was to lighten the depressing atmosphere in the room. Donnie let out a nervous laugh.

Tonika's countenance however, remained down trodden. From the looks on the two women faces, he soon realized his jovial teasing was anything but welcomed.

Even Etta Mae was taken aback, but the only way he knew to help was to keep his friend laughing.

"Laughter does a heart merry. At least that's what it says in Proverbs 15:13. "A merry heart makes a cheerful countenance."

"Ooo . . . honey, I'm scared of you." The proud wife said to her Bible knowledgeable husband.

"Don't worry, be happy . . . hoo, a hoo, hoo, hoo, a hoo a hoo . . ." Donnie sang as he basked in his newly acquired glory.

This was Donnie's outlook on life. He had found refuge under the shelter of laughter many times.

He just couldn't honestly believe that Josh would abandon his family like that. No real man would do that.

But, it appeared his world and Josh's world was totally different.

"Hey, Boo . . . you know us gals have our ways when it comes to you men; don't we Tonika?"

"Huh . . . what are you saying Etta Mae?" Tonika asked.

"I'm saying . . . do you think that's how Eve got Adam to bite that apple?"

"O' I don't know . . . it could be ya know. And you do know what head men think with."

"Oh, here we go! Now you two instigators are messing with my man Adam." Donnie said.

He proceeded to push his golf gear into the living room into a corner.

"What's Adam done to you two instigators?" Donnie said as he returned to the women.

"My friend, in case you didn't know it by now, all men are fair game. Even your boy Adam." Tonika said, fully realizing what Etta Mae was trying to do.

"Well that's my cue to exit, because it sounds like man bashing time. So I'm just gon a make like ya friend's old-man and disappear. Now if you two ladies will excuse me."

Broad smiles spread across the two faces. Their plan had worked.

"Whew! And I had better hit the shower too." Donnie lifted his shirt and sniffed his underarms. "I worked up a sweat pounding my clubs on the ground today and I'm all sweaty."

"Pee-yew! Yes you do, and please do it quickly!" Tonika said, holding her nose.

Tonika and Etta Mae used their hands to fan their faces as Donnie leaned towards them with one exposed underarm.

"Go on honey!" Etta Mae said as she pushed her husband away with her forearm.

"Ew! You smell like a musk ox marking his territory." Tonika joined in.

"No, what you smell is the scent of a man that's in his own home." Donnie countered. "Is it enough to drive you away?"

"And did you win Last Comic Bombing?"

"Okay, you two, quit it. And go take your shower, honey . . . please!"

"Oka-ay already . . . women folk, I swear. A fellow can't even be au natu-rel in his own home."

Donnie pecked his wife on the cheek on his way out of the room.

"See ya in a little bit, babe. Then we'll discuss what's for dinner. Tomika, you won't be here when I get back will ya?"

"I surely hope that wasn't your last wish, my brother."

"Oh, and honey, be sure to let my sister know she had a phone call."

Etta Mae proceeded over to the refrigerator.

"Tonika, do you want something else to drink?"

"Sure! I could go for a nice, cold one."

Donnie lifted the sweaty shirt over his head, as he walked down the hallway.

He stopped in front of the guestroom and gently knocked on the door.

"Hello . . . Dee?"

"Come in." Dee said, awakening out of a fitful nap. He opened the door just a crack.

"Oh! I'm sorry, I didn't know you were sleeping but I just wanted to let you know . . . I guess your hubby, called for ya earlier."

"*What* . . . Damien called here? And why did you say you guess? Either he did, or he didn't."

"Now just calm down, all I know is that the phone rang; I answered it, but the caller wouldn't say who he was.

He just asked if you were here. So, I-I mean that is, your sister naturally assumed it was your husband."

"O' that man has some balls calling me!" Dee fumed.

"Why shouldn't he call you? Wait a minute . . . do you mean you didn't let your husband know where you were going?"

Donnie threw the reeking shirt around his neck and stepped fully into the room.

"You care to tell me what's going on?"

Dee sat up in the bed, and smoothed the strands of hair that had dislodged from her up-do. An exaggerated sigh escaped her lips.

"Oh, Brother-in-law, how do I begin? More importantly, where do I begin?"

"How about starting from the beginning?" He said sitting on the edge of the bed. "Do you want to talk? I got time."

As Donnie sat down, Dee caught a whiff of his underarms and thought to herself.

"I'll sure have to make this quick so I don't prolong my boy's shower."

She reclined as far back as possible, and began to tell her woes.

Chapter Eight

"Uh umm." Etta Mae cleared her throat at her friend's request for a beer. "I was thinking more like lemonade, or a soda, Missy."

Tonika had really wanted, and desperately needed a cold brew, but was willing to accept the lemonade.

"Well . . . okay, a nice cold lemonade then. But a beer did sound more refreshing."

"I bet it did."

Etta Mae resolved to give her hurting friend the beer she so obviously craved. After all, she deserved it.

"Oops, sorry my friend, but my hubby took the last one. And it looks like we're all out of lemonade too. Darn! But I know you drink cola, so here.

"Girlie, you know me so well."

"And don't I know it . . . besides that's all there is other than tea." She handed her friend a can of cola. "I truly must go grocery shopping like soon!"

"Thanks." Tonika took a long swig of the cold sweet liquid, savoring its goodness.

Just then her cell phone buzzed, she picked it up and read a text message.

"Oh, that's Ashad saying he was about to leave."

"How's my sweet boy?" Etta Mae asked. "Toni, you've sure done a good job raising him."

"Thanks . . . but without you . . . let's just say, you both were life savers."

"You're welcome, and it was truly our pleasure." Etta Mae said. "Especially, since it doesn't look as if we'll be grandparents ourselves anytime soon."

"Oh, don't fret my friend, maybe you'll get that call one day soon from Janet."

"One can only hope. But I was emphatically told by my beautiful daughter that she and Geoffrey wanted to enjoy each other before starting a family. And not to mention, enjoy Hawaii as well!"

"Now I can understand that. They're entitled." Tonika said."

"Yes, they certainly are, but try telling the Don that. He wants 'em to hurry and be quick about it."

The two shared a hearty laugh.

"You know, we mentioned my girl Eve earlier. Etta Mae said after they had sat quietly, contemplating.

"There has to be something to that you know."

"Umm." Tonika swallowed the sip of cola. "To be truthful, I hadn't honestly given it much thought. But where're you going with it?"

"Oh, it's just that the old girl put one over on us women, is all. Don't you think?"

"Oh . . . I see what you mean. I-I guess."

"Just think about it, Tonika. She must've been something out of the ordinary. She even got Adam to go against El Shaddai."

"Humph, well if you ask me, it wouldn't be too nifty for her sorry butt to be around here at this point.

"A lot of women would just love to get their hands around that old neck of hers."

"Boo!" Out of nowhere an incarnated apparition appeared in the room.

The women were frightened beyond belief. They jumped up and clutched each other tightly.

"Whoa-a! Et-ta, who's t-that?" Tonika trembled in fear.

"We-ll . . ." Etta Mae began to offer the shaking woman the only explanation she knew.

"I k-know it's not Wilma Flintstone so it has to be Miss Eve."

"W-Why do you say th-that, E-Etta?"

"Who else would walk around in animal skin in this type weather?"

Etta Mae looked toward the manifested figure with apprehension. She concluded a portal had indeed been opened into the spirit realm. Well so be it, but for some strange reason, the fear she felt at first had begun to dissipate.

Maybe, just maybe, this strange creature had been sent for a special reason.

"Hold it together ladies, fear not, for, I bring you good tidings!"

Eve offered an exhilarating greeting. She actually found the two women somewhat amusing.

"I believe that's how the angels say it when they pop in for a visit."

"Good tidings?" Tonika finally found her bearings and asked. "From where and from what? Who exactly are you?"

"Tonika, I told you." Etta Mae said.

"Questions, questions, questions! Why I'm Eve of course, and exactly where do you think I'm from? To-mi-ka! Eve swaggeringly answered.

The startled woman's eyes widened at the brazen liberty that had been taken with her name.

"I heard you two discussing me, so I thought I might pay you a little visit. You know . . . I decided it was time to tell my side of the story."

"Wait a minute!" Etta Mae shouted. "You said you heard us discussing you? How and what exactly did you hear?"

"I obviously heard enough to make me want to pop in on you two."

"Oh, and who knew it would bring about all this?"

"Darling, I'm surprised at you. Etta Mae, have you forgotten Hebrews 12:1 you read this morning? "Therefore, we're surrounded by such a great cloud of witnesses . . ."

"You mean you were the one that caused my Bible to turn to that passage?"

"Well . . . let's just say . . . as a cloudy witness . . ."

"Now you do have to know we're not exactly in the habit of talking to ghosts." Tonika retorted. "It just ain't natural!"

"I wouldn't go so far as to say that, madam."

"And my name by the way is with an n, To-ni-ka!"

The irritated neighbor adamantly pointed out.

"No . . . It-ain't-natural." Eve mockingly said. *"Etta Mae said it this morning. "God is doing a new thing."*

"And just exactly what new thing is God doing?" Tonika wanted to know.

"Well . . . For one thing, He's simply putting the super on your natural. And ladies, I'm not talking hair."

Eve tugged at the crown of natural locks that adorned her head.

"You get it, natural?"

She laughed at her play on words. But the senseless humor received only blank stares.

"Besides the fact of you guys talking to ghosts like it's no big deal there's nothing strange about my being here

Eve added. What's that box you all call t-tele-vision?"

Yes, a television, tell-a-vision." Etta Mae interpreted.

"Okay, that thing! You can almost always find some undaunted hero going into a haunted house. The first thing they say is, "Speak to me, if you're in here."

"Yeah, yeah, and your point is?" Tonika said to Eve. "We know what you're implying? It's not as if we're dumb, you know."

Eve stood her ground with the arrogant human. She placed both hands on her hips, and emphatically stated.

"Missy, the dumb thing about it all is that God showed you where He stood on all this in Deuteronomy 18:10 "Whoever practices witchcraft, sorcery, or who is a medium, a psychic or the like, is detestable to Him."

"And you said that to say what?" Tonika asked.

"That you hard headed humans, thinking you know everything . . . what do you do? You go and do just the opposite."

"It's all done in the name of science, thank you."

"Tell that to your Maker."

"Well, I won't bother Him, but now that you're here, it's my opportunity do what I said I'd do." Tonika said. She stood and advanced toward the materialized specter.

"And that was to whip your butt!"

"Tonika! Girl, sit down!" Etta Mae demanded. "And calm down! It does not take all that."

The quarrelsome damsel reluctantly returned to her seat. Satisfied that a crisis had been avoided, Etta Mae then said to Eve.

"So, girlfriend, since you're here, we'll let you say your piece, because you have a lot of explaining to do."

"Woman, spirit, whatever you are!" Tonika shouted, before Eve could speak.

"You don't have a side, all I know is, you blew it for all us women, and that's the bottom line!"

"Geez, could your pot boil any hotter?"

"What do you know about a boiling pot?" Etta Mae wanted to know. "You mean you had a pot to boil?"

Eve laughed, but watched the grouchy neighbor closely. She wasn't too concern with the animosity the distraught soul displayed toward her. Usually, that type often needed to vent their frustration at something, or someone. So, by all rights, it may as well be against her, the Mother of all Living.

"Girl, uh, I meant Eve. Just tell us why you did what you did and what was the reason behind all of it?" Etta Mae proceeded to ask.

"What can I say? Other than, there was no excuse."

"My thoughts exactly!" Etta Mae said. "Honey, if anybody ever had it made, it had to be you."

"And you don't think I know that all I had to do was just wander about that beautiful garden that our beautiful Creator provided for Adam and me."

Eve walked away from the women, absorbed in what she'd lost, but the moment of melancholy was interrupted.

"Yeah, she didn't even have to cook, clean, do laundry or anything.

That's probably why she got into trouble in the first place." Tonika ranted on.

"You know they say an "idol mind is the devil's workshop," and from the looks of it, her mind was pretty idol."

"Well, I wouldn't go so far as to say that, Miss Thang, but you're correct in one thing though."

"I am? And what might that be?"

"You were correct in the fact that all I had to do was to pick a plant and eat it. Food, water, companionship . . . speaking of which, that was why I was created you know, to be a companion to your boy Adam. I was supposed to be his help meet."

"And I would say you helped him meet alright, helped his butt right on out of that glorious garden!"

Etta Mae slapped a high-five with her neighbor. Eve rolled her eyes and chose to ignore the women.

"After all, I am . . . bone of his bone, and flesh of his flesh. But no-o! Your girl messed up! I just had to go and wander off that day, being nosy.

Now, you know that's where you girls get that from . . . Me!"

"Now I know you're lying, I didn't get anything from you." Tonika said, defensively. "I'm not nosy! I'm, or we're merely observant. Now, am I right about it, girlfriend?"

"Yes, we're merely observant." Etta Mae said in agreement. "We observe this, and we observe that, and if that's not being nosy, then I don't know what is?" She said, as she slapped her open hand on the table. "Now, Tonika, would you just shush?"

"Yes, Toni, shush!"

Eve had wanted to say that to the annoying human herself, and was overjoyed when Etta Mae had done just that.

"Then that ole wily serpent appeared in that tree and got the best of me. He probably had been watching me the whole while!

Come telling me; "Sssssss . . . now you know God is withholding something from you and Adam. There is something he doesn't want you to know . . . Ssssssss."

Now you know my ears perked up, don't you?"

"Your *ears* perked up? Sweetie, you're referring to a talking snake. I know what would have perked up alright . . . my perked up ass-ociation would have hauled butt right out of there." Tonika adamantly stated.

"Now, why would you run Miss Scaredy-Cat?" It was only a little ole snake."

"Well honey, around here snakes don't talk."

This time Etta Mae is the one to stand to her feet.

"I'm sure I do not have to tell you . . . if I ever ran up on a live snake, *honey,* he would soon be a dead snake, because Mama does not play that."

The women laughed at Etta Mae's demonstration of stomping on a snake.

"Now I know you women aren't scared of a little old snake. Not when I see you wrapping them all around your neck and dance with them."

'Un, un, I ain't the one! You won't catch Sistah-Girl dancing with a stupid snake!" Etta Mae said.

"But then look who I'm talking to, Miss Erie Etta and her side kick, Miss Timid Toni."

"What did you call us?" Tonika asked, demanding to know. She rose to approach Eve once again.

"Etta Mae, you hear that? I know you're lying now! You haven't seen me wrapping no snake round this neck!"

"Oh, just hold your horses." Eve said, backing up. *"Did I say you? Well, I meant women in general. And do the both of you know you're supposed to put enmity between yourself and the serpent?"*

The ladies shook their heads in recognition.

Now please, allow me to continue."

"Good, but let's clarify one thing. I'm not touching anybody's slimy snake! Uugh!" Tonika shuddered and sat down.

"Thank you, Miss G. Now if you remember, little ole me was pulled from Adam's side, you know his rib. So I was a big part of the man,

you understand. It's like this . . . I represent Adam's conscious side; that is his soul.

"You what?" Etta Mae inquired. "His soul, you say?"

"I'm surprised at you, Bible-worm. Yes, his soul. Your soul is your feelings, your thinker, your emotions, and your will power. And, even still, your chooser. You mean you didn't know that?"

"Well I know it now." Etta Mae said.

"Good! I'm glad you do, because old Satan knew it too, and he knew just who to come to. Me!"

"Yeah, and you lost your soul, and everyone else's, right then and there!" Tonika said.

"Hel-lo! Let's just say the snake piqued my curiosity. Okay Missy?"

The ladies finally settled down and gave Eve the chance to tell a large chunk of her tale.

"Why, that lying piece of . . . well, I don't have to spell it out for you, do I?"

"No, we can sort of garner what happened."

"He was hanging out in this beautiful tree loaded with delectable fruit. Needless to say, I bit into the fruit, but do you know nothing happened. Though somehow, I knew I'd messed up.

Now, you know I couldn't be in this mess alone. If I were going down, Brother-Man was going down with me!

So, I put on my best womanly charm, and when Adam approached he couldn't resist. He bit too! And now both our eyes were opened. Right off, we both realized we were naked."

Eve seductively swayed her hips.

"Now, for the first time, Adam looked at me with lust in his eyes."

"Girl, quit jiving." Tonika said with disbelief. "You mean to tell me, there you are standing there butt naked and your man never drank you in with his eyes? Come on now, Miss Evie."

"Hold up, Tonika, she could be right you know." Etta Mae

said. "What does the Bible say about lust? That it was a sin, right? And because of what was done, she and Adam's eyes had now been opened to that sin."

"Okay, I get it. They were innocent in their love for each other before then."

"Now, don't forget Miss Etta, we were husband and wife; so our lust wasn't a sin."

"You're so right, Eve girl! My bad." Etta Mae admitted.

"Apology accepted . . . Now I know many of you have often wondered why Adam also ate of the fruit."

Eve paced back and forth. She paused ever so often to drive home her point. Tonika and Etta Mae hung on to her every word.

"Ladies, you see Adam represented the 'spirit part of man. Remember, he was made in the image of God, who is Spirit and who is also the very embodiment of Love." Eve hugged herself before continuing.

"Now you see, because Adam was made in the image of God, and because Adam loved me, he chose not to separate from me, and leave his woman hanging, or his soul per se.

So, my Boo, as you say Etta Mae, bit into that fruit, bringing us three back together again. Body, soul and spirit. Otherwise, where would you two be?"

With the snap of her fingers the two women became more alert. Etta Mae and Tonika looked at each other and simply shrugged their shoulders.

"But, ladies, do you know what the drawback of it all was?" Eve began to sob.

"No, we couldn't begin to guess." Etta Mae said. "What was the drawback, you poor thing."

"The drawback of it all was that even though Adam and me were together. We were now separated from our glorious Creator."

"Please don't cry." Etta Mae said. She extended her arms to offer comfort, but thought better of it and quickly pulled back.

"I'm sure you didn't. And by the way, it's Adam and I."

"Oh, so now all of a sudden, we're into using proper English. So what was up with your word ain't being thrown around so freely?"

"Etta! What are you doing? You don't have to pity her. She probably knew exactly what she was doing all along!"

However, Etta Mae was convinced differently and seemingly had an epiphany moment.

"Tonika girl, it makes sense though. I never thought of it like that before. I've always wondered why Adam went against his Creator."

"I can't believe you fell for that cheap display of humility." Tonika cajoled.

Eve watched the two ladies out of the corner of her eye. She fully realized the troubled neighbor was a force to be reckoned with.

"Wow! You see, you learned something new today!" Etta Mae grabbed hold of Tonika's arm. "And I hate to say it, but I'm glad she came."

"Well, if you ask me, there was no choice to be made."

Tonika used her hands as if they were weighing scales.

"Eve; God, God; Eve. Nope! No comparison!"

Eve flippantly addressed the clueless woman.

"Okay, Miss Lady, here's a question for you. If you think the decision was that easy, then why don't more of you choose Him today?"

"What do you mean by that?" Etta Mae asked.

"Yes, why did you say that? You hear us crying all the time; God bless America! We are a Bible believing nation."

"Are you two serious, or just clueless? I believe you also have what you call your atheists and your agnostics in your Bible believing nation as well."

Etta Mae lowered her head. She didn't need to be reminded of that very fact.

"Ummph, I have to admit girlfriend, you're so right." She said.

They each pondered the question. Then Tonika made what she considered an amazing observation.

"But do you know what's funny about all that?"

"What?"

"Yes, what" Etta Mae asked.

"That that very same group of 'A' list people, those agnostics and atheists, share in the very same blessings we believers do in this nation. Now, do you see how good our God is?"

"I see what you mean, Toni. The unbelievers share the blessings of God, just as much as the believers." Etta Mae concluded.

"You know it, because He rain on the just, as well as the unjust! And here's another one for 'you." Eve added.

"The sin wasn't brought about because of the fruit. No . . . the sin came about from our disobedience. The very fact that we took the 'serpent's word over His Word was what did it! So there you have it, so to speak, in a nutshell."

Eve was pleased with her ability to finally stomp the belligerent humans.

"Now, I don't have an answer for you there." Etta Mae said. "All I can say is you two sure had some balls."

Tonika shook her head in agreement. Etta Mae's statement confused the non-human.

"Oh, you don't know about having balls?" Tonika asked.

"What she means is; you two hardheads had some nerves . . . guts! You know, intestinal fortitude to go against the Almighty like you did!"

Eve stood in silence, with her head bowed. No words were said between either of them for a long time.

Chapter Nine

"Donnie, you're a man . . . I, uh, I mean a man's man. Right?" Dee stammered, suddenly feeling uncomfortable.

"Hell ye-ahh! Duhhh! Why . . . why do you ask that?"

"Oh, I'm sorry, I didn't mean for you to think I was questioning your manhood."

"Oh, I'm okay with it." Donnie said with a deeper voice than necessary.

"Well, it's just that I can't fathom why a man would want to look at another man."

"Good grief, so that's it! Don't tell me your husband is on the DL? The Down Low."

The look on Dee's face answered for her silence.

"My Lord! Delilah."

"Yep, you got it."

"Da-amn! That's some deep shi . . . uh, sorry." Donnie uttered apologetically.

"Who're you telling? And the way I found out was . . . well, I'm not ready to give details just yet. I'm still coming to grips with it myself."

Donnie, understandably, didn't press for further details. He could sense how disturbing it must be for his sister-in-law.

"Oh, I understand, and believe me when I say I don't think I could stomach it anyhow. E-eww!" He shuddered at the thought.

"Thanks for understanding, because I wouldn't wish anything like what happened to me on my worst enemy."

"So what are you going to do?" He asked with genuine concern. "I mean with your marriage and all?"

"I don't know. I told my sister I was divorcing, but truthfully, I honestly don't know.

I obviously love my husband, but I needed to get away, to clear my head."

"Well, you can stay here as long as you like. And your sister . . . what are you going to tell her?"

"I don't know . . . I feel so much like a failure, and I don't want her to worry about me."

"Have you told her anything besides you are getting a divorce?"

"No, I haven't, but I was about to this morning."

Dee raised her hand to signal a stop.

"But just believe me when I tell you, I dread the moment."

"I'm sure she's wondering." Donnie added.

"I know; I know . . . so you don't have to tell me. Dang! I'm sure she is."

"Al-though, she's surprising me with just how patient she's being. It's out of her character not to push to get to the bottom of an issue." He said.

"I know how she is, and then there's her gal pal."

"What was that? Now Dee, I have to come to my wife's defense. I'm sure she's just giving you time to sort through things. So don't let that hinder you from going to her . . . promise?"

"Okay already, I promise. Geez!"

She reluctantly agreed then thoughtfully admitted.

"You're right, but this is just not something I want, or think I can talk to her about."

"I don't know why not."

"Bro-law, you know her righteous stance on everything." She searched his face for understanding. "You understand, don't you?"

"I admit it has got to be hard for you, but the ball is in your court."

"It's just that my sanctimonious sister would want to know every detail, and I'm not ready for that! Nobody knows the hell I'm going through right now!"

"Calm down, please. I tell you what . . . you sleep on it a little longer, and then we'll see."

He rose from the bed, but before he reached the door, he said to his sister-in-law.

"Say what you want, but my baby has a very big heart!"

"Yes, she does at that, and she always has." Dee said.

She smiled as she got up from the bed to give her dear brother-in-law a loving hug.

"Thanks for listening. Now go take your shower, please." They both laughed.

"You're certainly welcome, that's what families are for. When you hurt we hurt."

"Thank you, Bro-law."

You're welcome, but my advice to you is not to keep it from your sister too much longer. Okay, Delilah?"

"Oh, there's Delilah again. Now that's serious, but I do promise."

Dee returned to the bed and closed her weary eyes.

"To-mor-row."

"Good." Donnie said and left the room.

Chapter Ten

"I still say, everyone's responsible for their own decisions, as well as their own actions." Etta Mae said, seizing the reins once again. "The Father only wants those who come to Him to come willingly."

Eve pondered the housewife's comment. She knew how deeply troubled the Father had become behind their senseless actions.

"Yes, and I can tell you truthfully, we hurt Him deeply. And it still hurts when one of his creations becomes eternally separated from Him."

"I don't know about you, but if I had the power to save the world I would." Etta Mae said, struggling to keep from crying. "I would do it, just to make Him happy again."

"Earth to Etta-a." said Tonika. "Hel-lo! Don't you remember? His Son already did that! You do remember how Christ shed His precious blood for you and for me, don't you? Even for that . . . her."

"Thank you Jesus! Praise the Lord!"

All three were caught up in a praise break.

"Yes, and thank you, I do remember. And He did it all just so no one would have to suffer the Second Death." Etta Mae declared. Eve shook her head in agreement.

"What's the Second Death?" Tonika inquired. "A person can only die once, right?

Now I do know that much. When you're dead, you're dead!"

"Oh, I see we've got ourselves a baby Christian, huh? But don't worry girlie, eyes are watching over you."

Eve looked at Tonika with an all-knowing grin and bent over to become eye level with her.

"What? Etta Mae, help me!"

"Oh girl, she just meant the eyes of God. Oh yes! And that cloud of witnesses she mentioned.

And Evie, you can rest assured on my friend's convergence. I'm making doubly sure of that."

"Very well then Miss Etta Mae. I was just checking. I made the statement only because I cared."

"Eve, y-you care?" Tonika sputtered.

"She cares!" The two women laughed unbelievingly.

"What?" You think I'm so cold hearted that I don't care about mankind?"

The perplexed look on the women's faces led her to say.

"Come on! I made the wrong choice once, and I certainly paid for it!"

"Uh hmm, excuse me, but I think we've all paid for it." Tonika interjected.

"So sue me, as you all say." Eve said. *"Even after my husband knew me, and I conceived again . . ."*

"Knew you? Tonika exclaimed. "You mean he didn't know who you were before? It was only the two of you, if I recall correctly."

"Tonika, if you would please . . ." Etta Mae said wearily. "It's just how they spoke in those days."

"Etta Mae I'm sure glad you can read me, or shall I say, read the Book."

She stole a glance at the clueless one. *"And just as the Creator said, I brought forth my first born in pain."*

She recalled the agony she had suffered in childbirth and doubled over in imaginary pain.

"Oh! The pain of it all!"

Her actions evoked no sign of sympathy from Tonika, who soon lost interest in Eve's excuses for her long ago actions.

As far as she was concerned she couldn't in any form, or fashion, vindicate herself from the trauma of child bearing with no amount of explanation.

Donnie headed toward his bedroom, greatly anticipating a hot shower. The voices he heard coming from the front of the house caused him to stop in his tracks. He turned and headed in their direction.

Tonika and his wife had been alone when he had left the room earlier.

Had someone come in while he and Dee were talking? With curiosity getting the better of him, Donnie silently tipped down the hall and peered into the room.

What he saw next caused him to fall back against the wall. He was startled beyond belief.

"I know you women curse me to this day." Eve lamented. *"Even I could kick myself."*

"Here let me do you the honors." Tonika lifted her foot from the floor.

Eve avoided the extended foot just in time as her gaze travelled into the hallway. There she caught sight of the frightened man and stared deep into his eyes.

"Who or better yet, what is that?" Donnie said under his breath. Beads of sweat ran down his temple.

A barefoot, statuesque, Nubian figure clad in unidentifiable animal skin strutted back and forth, talking with his wife and Tonika.

The far set eyes were enhanced with extended black lashes. Hair of coarse ropes fell mid-waist down her back. A tilted nose protruded from a gaunt face of wisdom that sat just above full, sensuous lips.

Ample breasts rose like two proud robins performing a mating ritual. All in all, the woman was something to behold.

"Wait a minute! Did I just hear them call her Eve?"

Nothing could have prepared the man for this moment. How could this be happening in his home?

Yep, there'd certainly been a supernatural breach of sorts like his wife had said this morning. But, the question is . . . why?

Donnie's assumption that the paranormal activity could play itself out when and wherever it desired had proven correct.

"Oh, don't be so hard on yourself Evie girl. It all worked out in the end. It was already known by your heavenly Father what you were up against from the beginning. And that was . . . Satan!"

"I know what you mean, Etta Mae."

Eve reflected on how much she liked the way the woman thought. She even decided to address the time she had remaining specifically to Etta Mae.

For the life of her, Tonika could not understand exactly how she had gotten caught up in this paranormal occurrence. She had only come over to her BFF's to cry on her shoulder.

"No need to worry, God didn't intend for us to live in sin forever. And like you said, the Father already had a way to redeem Adam and me. Thank you LORD!"

After the praise break she addressed the ladies once again.

"Ah ladies . . . can I ask you something?"

"That depends on what it is." Tonika. said, with eyes narrowed.

"Can you find it in your hearts to forgive me? After all, I am truly, truly, sorry."

This was all said of course with false humility. Eve's eyes were drawn to the bowl of fruit on the table. Their eyes followed her gaze as she reached for an apple.

"Can I have one of these?"

Tonika slapped at her hands.

"May I have?" Etta Mae corrected.

"Oh, for goodness sakes! May I have?"

She then took a hefty bite of the luscious fruit, savoring its sweetness.

"Mmmmm . . . oh by the way, who said it was an apple I bit anyway?"

"What?" Tonika asked.

"Yeah . . . what? This time it was Etta Mae.

"Now you two ladies just wrap your heads around that one."

Eve then turned to wink at Donnie and faded into oblivion, and left the women to ponder the bombshell she had just dropped.

Etta Mae and Tonika sat as if dumbfounded and stared into space. Tonika, the first to gather her composure got up from the table.

It seemed to the formidable male in the hallway as if the specter had looked deep into the very core of his being.

He took a deep intake of breath, and shrunk back in fear. A wet puddle that had just happened to form in the exact spot where he had been sitting made it necessary for a hasty retreat.

He reached the bedroom door, and shut it with a pronounced force before he gave way to the mounted fear.

"Yo-owww!" Oh man, that was some scary shit out there!" He just couldn't seem to stop his knees from shaking.

"I can't believe it."

Donnie's mind traveled back to what had just happened.

Oh, help me, Jesus! I saw it with my own eyes, but I still can't believe it. He thought of how his wife and Tonika appeared to have been lulled into some sort of a trance.

Surely by now, Dee would've sensed something. Why hadn't she come out of her room to investigate?

But he would deal with the perplexity of it all later, once he got cleaned up.

He stripped off his wet clothing and jumped into the refreshing shower.

"What was that noise?" The sleeping beauty queen rose from the bed and went to the door.

"It sounded like someone yelling." Dee opened the door a crack and peered out.

The sound had come from the master bedroom. She was about to close the door again when she heard the voices of her sister and neighbor.

Dee stood there for a moment trying to decide if she should go out. Finally, she closed the door with her thoughts on how and what to tell her sister still fresh in her mind.

Perhaps, I need to talk with someone else first, like a pastor maybe, before making any decisions.

The chat with her brother-in-law had helped a little. He hadn't been too judgmental.

What little she had told her brother-in-law had shocked him. But alas, it's the way of the world today.

She approached the bed once again. The decision of what she would do had been made.

I'll just finish my nap and later I'll take a walk around the neighborhood for some clean air.

Then maybe I'll look for a church whose doors might just happen to be open. I can't believe I said that. I really must be desperate.

But . . . yes, that's what I'll do. After all, this thing is too big for me. Maybe it will take a man of the cloth to make everything plain.

With her mind in a well-deserved state of euphoria, Dee drifted off to sleep once again.

Chapter Eleven

"I can't believe what just happened!" Tonika lashed out. "That heifer just pops out just like she popped in. "Can you find it in your heart to forgive me?" What nerve!"

Etta Mae looked on with disinterest, not caring to add to the charade.

"And did you see how flippant she was acting? And just what was that last comment about? Everyone knows it was an apple she took from that tree.

Tonika looked to Etta Mae for confirmation. "It was . . . wasn't it?"

The befuddled neighbor slightly shoved her seemingly traumatized cohort to bring her out of her stupor.

"What do you think the fruit was?" Tonika paced back and forth.

"Huh, what?"

"The fruit Etta Mae, the fruit, what was it?"

"The fruit . . . the fruit, now let's see." Etta Mae pondered the matter.

"Hmmm, I don't exactly know. Maybe it was a fig. The Bible does say Adam and Eve covered themselves with a fig leaf."

"A fig you think, are you sure?"

"Look, all I know is, there's a lot of talk about fig trees in the Bible, but I haven't heard of, not to my knowledge anything about apple trees."

"Fig, apple, turnip!" Tonika razzed. "What's the point?"

"Of course I could be wrong. So don't quote me on it. I just might have to research that one."

"And old Evie-Eve should be sorry, as much pain as I went through giving birth to that nine-pound big-headed boy of mine."

"Tonika, would you get a grip, get a hold of yourself!"

"Etta Mae, I'm serious. And you ought to be glad you stopped me from getting my hands on her. I would have rung her flipping neck!"

Etta Mae looked on her friend with amusement.

"Your boy did have a big old head."

They each found that statement hilarious, and filled the room with hysterics.

After which, Etta Mae voiced a concern that had just entered her mind.

"Sa-ay girl, I wonder if any more unwanted guests will pop in today." She eerily surveyed the room.

"I certainly hope not, I don't think I could stand it. And besides that, don't be laughing at my sweet pea. That's my little munchkin, big head and all."

"You know it does hurt pushing those little boogers out into the world. But once you look into those little faces you forget about all the pain you went through. Now am I right?" Etta Mae added.

The broadest smile spread across her face by just thinking about the birth of her daughter Janet. Yes, she could truly identify with the sentiments of her friend.

Each time they spoke with their daughter, Granddaddy wanna be always anticipated hearing, "surprise, we're pregnant!"

"Speaking of which, maybe I should call my husband. He should be out of the shower by now."

"Please let Donnie Leroy stay in that shower as long as possible."

"Now leave my Boo alone."

An annoying fly had constantly buzzed Etta Mae's head. She absentmindedly swatted at it.

Tonika took note of Etta Mae's plight with the annoying insect.

"Girl what is with you and that fly?"

"With me, what's up with it, and where is that darn fly swatter when you need it?"

"It's probably where you last swatted your husband with it."

"Stop it girl, you're too much. Hey, Tonika do you know what?"

"No, I can't say I know what but I know who." Tonika hysterically laughed at her own unwarranted joke.

"Now you know you can be a fool when you wanna be." Etta Mae said with amusement. "But you know I didn't feel quite right having that close encounter of the third kind pop up like that."

"I know exactly what you mean, because I didn't either." Tonika said. "Now you know my knees were knocking the whole time."

A tingling sensation ran down Tonika's spine. She shuddered in her seat.

"I know they did but you soon got over it, and then you became a tyrant."

"I did, didn't I? Wonder where all that courage came from?"

"I don't know, but what do you think would happen if we started talking about you know who?"

"Who?"

"Now I thought you said you knew who, silly." Etta Mae laughed and said. "Beelzebub, the Lord of the flies that's who."

"O' my, for the sake of all that is holy, honey, please do not bring him up."

Etta Mae recalled what she had heard at Bible study. The discussion on Mark 3:22. The Pharisees accused Jesus of driving out demons by the power of Beelzebub the prince of demons.

It had felt creepy discussing it then, and it felt even creepier now that the morning's weird encounter had occurred. And there was still that annoying fly.

"If you don't! Now the darn thing is buzzing my head!"

The annoying visitor would only light long enough to send each woman swinging with both hands. Then the flying nuisance would lift off. This went on for quite some time.

The frustrated keeper of her castle made a makeshift fly swatter out of a rolled newspaper.

"Here! Let me have a go at him."

Whack

The fly however had sensed his impending doom and reacted just in time by flying a short distance out of harm's way.

"Ouch!"

The weapon of choice had missed its target, but had landed solidly on Tonika's head.

"Darn! I missed it!"

"Yes, you did, but you gave me a concussion in the process. Dang, it!"

The unfortunate receiver of the wayward blow gingerly rubbed the pulsating area.

"I'm sorry, here let mama kiss it and make it all bet-ter."

"No, thanks, that won't be necessary."

Tonika put out a hand to block the unwelcomed gesture.

"Well, don't say I didn't try." Etta Mae said.

"Yes, you tried, but wasn't that creepy how that thing kept going from you and then to me?"

The creepy invader eventually, lifted off its safety perch and flew out of the room.

"Something wasn't quite right about it, I know that." Etta Mae said. "I didn't want to spook you, so I didn't say anything."

"Well, honey, you can consider me spooked. That was scary! And it may've been my imagination, but I could've sworn that thing looked me dead in my eye."

"I know, right! I think it's time to bring out the smoking gun." Etta Mae said. She rose up from the table like a woman on a mission.

"And that would be?"

"Why, the B-I-B-L-E! And not only that, but I'm going to hit that fly with a double whammy!"

"Oh my! That thing's going to rue the day he messed with Etta Mae Collins Smith!"

"Now you're right about that!"

The spiritual crusader anointed every surface with extra virgin olive oil and prayed as she went.

"There! That should really hit the pest where it really hurts."

"You sure had it coming, messing with the demon buster in her own home, I tell you that, you dumb fly." Tonika excitedly added.

"You know after all this I think I need to get some fresh air. What about you?" Etta Mae said.

"Yes Lord! What do you have in mind?"

"I don't know about you, but nothing would clear my head better than a good old shopping spree. So, what do you say we do some damage in Kolkrofts today?"

"Girl, you're on. I'll be right back!"

Tonika managed to jump up from her seat despite having wobbly legs and headed for the door.

Etta Mae looked toward the bedroom.

"I won't bother my honey; hopefully, he has taken his shower by now and is probably fast asleep. Besides the fact, he'll warn me not to spend his newly disclosed raise."

Etta Mae chuckled and decided to scribble a note to inform him of her whereabouts. Plus she knew her sister would be long asleep after complaining of being disturbed this morning.

"Honey, I'm gone!"

She retrieved her purse from the sofa table and quietly left the house. She slid easily into the sleek gray 2000 Audi S4.

Tonika ran from across the street a little winded. Now satisfied her son had left for his practice, she settled into the passenger seat.

The supple luxury charcoal gray leather seats readily molded to their frames.

The captain at the helm of the wheel manipulated the sound system from the steering column and located her favorite station.

The Twilight Mall in nearby Ragnarok, was their anticipated destination and was a fifteen minute drive.

Surprisingly, few words were exchanged between the car's occupants.

They were each deep in thought and neither wanted to break the emotionally charged silence.

Along with the supernatural visit by Eve this morning, Dee's situation was a point of stress for Etta Mae.

Her friend struggled with the decision of whether or not she wanted to share her marriage turmoil.

She had been about ready to cry on her compassionate neighbor's shoulder when she'd first gone over, but that had all changed.

Tonika nervously glanced over at her dear friend, desperately wanting to release the tightness in her chest. But the pink element that once moved so freely now cleaved to the roof of her mouth.

The luxury sedan sliced effortlessly through the air like a bullet destined for its target.

After a seemingly endless ride, they finally pulled into the east parking lot of the Twilight Mall.

The ladies exited and aimlessly surveyed the parking lot dotted with late model vehicles. Even a Hummer or two were situated here and there.

"Boy, you sure couldn't tell it by this parking lot full of new cars that we're in a recession." Tonika said.

"Not when you have ole C.C. a recession doesn't matter."

"What does a gospel singer have to do with all these fine cars?"

"No girl!" Etta Mae said. "C. C., credit cards!"

"Oh, okay, I'm with you now."

"Look at it this way; as long as your credit's good you can have the world."

The two women shared a much needed laugh.

"Child I need to go into Peony's. Ashad is growing out of clothes faster than a weed in a compost heap."

Tonika adjusted the strap of her shoulder bag and looked up in time to see a familiar female figure hurrying their way.

Chapter Twelve

A feral cat had been seen prowling the meticulously landscaped back yard. A stealthy figure that stood watch under his corkscrew willow tree was primed and ready for the culprit. Colorful Japanese koi tranquilly swam in the stocked pond, oblivious to any pending danger.

However, Donnie's vigil was cut short as a grumbling stomach made its wants known. One last inspection of his prized fish and the ravenous guard made his way inside.

The jubilant gardener looked forward to an enjoyable, relaxing, Saturday afternoon alone.

His wife had long since left for the mall. He hadn't even gotten a chance to discuss the excitement of the morning with either her or his sister-in-law.

Etta Mae had left before he could come out of the bedroom, but had left a note to say that she and Tonika had gone shopping.

After Dee had awakened and showered, he'd simply put a key in her hand and had told her to have a pleasant walk. He had warned her to be careful and to stay alert.

Admittedly, Donnie was all too eager to settle into his familiar routine of watching his favorite television show, *Where Angels Tread*.

His mind still couldn't seem to shake the eerie occurrence that had happened earlier.

What was the world coming to? Paranormal activity everywhere, spirits popping up at whim.

Donnie mentally recalled the image of a book he'd casually browsed while waiting for Etta Mae to finalize a purchase at Binders Christian Bookstore.

One book in particular had caught his eye, *Heaven, It's A Trip!* He recalled being so intrigued by the book's title that he grabbed it off the shelf and skimmed a few pages.

The book's cover was so surreal and depicted a picture of billowy white cumulus clouds sat against the bluest sky.

Donnie had read the caption on the back cover. A woman had had an out of body experience with the Lord. On her supernatural journey she was given a brief glimpse of hell.

The woman had stated she hadn't been afraid because the Lord was with her, but was saddened to see so many people she'd known in that horrible place.

Jesus had then escorted her to heaven. She had stated the immense beauty of the place was indescribable.

Donnie had been skeptical about the woman's supposedly visitation and had replaced the book on the shelf.

His thoughts returned to the moment at hand. According to the clock on the wall, it would be a race of time if he wanted to grab a bite and catch his special episode.

But try as he might, he just couldn't seem to get the picture of the phenomenal woman from this morning out of his head.

It has to be all the accelerated interests in the paranormal that these weird things are happening. We just keep messing with those hants. People know they ought-a quit.

Donnie shuddered and looked around the spacious kitchen.

"Who ya gon a call? Ghost Busters!" He laughed in the face of his uneasiness.

After he had washed his hands in the sink, Donnie tangoed his way to the refrigerator.

"Ya ought 'a be starting somethin . . . ought 'a be startin somethin . . . Un, un, un, un, um. Mm, mm, mm, mm, mm."

A buzzing fly perched itself on top of the chrome finished double door refrigerator as Donnie peered inside.

The famished man visually began to check off the necessary ingredients needed to make his Donnie Detonator sub sandwich. He personally claimed full rights to the overstuffed concoction.

"Let's see here . . . cotto salami, honey glazed ham, smoked turkey breast, shredded lettuce, and tomatoes. Check and . . . check!"

He reached for a little jar way back in the fridge. Donnie lifted the lid but just as quickly closed it.

"Ooh, boy, my little secret ingredient, you are a tad too ripe." He quickly searched the refrigerator shelves and found other ingredients.

"Alright then, dill pickles, yumm . . . banana peppers, green pepper, onions, cheddar and Swiss cheese, and . . . ah yes, my pretty little Pro-vo-lone."

He placed all the trappings of his mouth watering delight on the counter and returned to the refrigerator for condiments.

"Now where is my special salad dressing?"

Donnie reached for his other secret ingredient hidden behind Etta Mae's homemade chicken salad.

"Come on baby you've hidden long enough."

He moved ketchup, olive bottles, and left over spaghetti in a plastic container, only to find the jar empty.

"What? It's empty! I can't believe it. Et-ta!" He shouted into the air. "I sure hope you're grocery shopping." The disappointed master sandwich maker picked up a jar of mustard instead.

"I guess this mustard will have to do. Darn, it just won't be the same."

Donnie eyed the mouthwatering chicken salad his wife had made for the women's auxiliary program.

He had watched her mix the sour cream, salad dressing, celery, onions, boiled eggs, pickle relish and other ingredients in with the cooled diced chicken. The salad was one of his wife's most coveted dishes at the church.

"Humph, I certainly don't want to hear Etta Mae's mouth, so unless I have a death wish I'd better not touch that salad."

The deli delight was finally constructed, all with heightened anticipation. A tall glass of sweetened iced tea was next on the menu.

The ravenous marauder made his way across the room pleased with his successful raid in the refrigerator.

He sat the food down and clicked on the television, poised to sit in his favorite leather recliner. Then suddenly the doorbell rang.

"Oh, man!" He said, irritated at being interrupted. "Now who could that be?"

Perhaps his sister-in-law had forgotten her key, but then he remembered he had personally placed it squarely in her palm.

"I don't know who it could be then, but I sure don't feel like being bothered."

The doorbell rang once again. Donnie turned down the volume. He looked first toward the door then back to the television and remained perfectly still.

Shucks, it's probably for Etta Mae anyway. Everyone I know is still on the golf course. Maybe, if I don't answer, whoever it is will go away.

Persistent knocking followed his assumption. An immense sigh escaped his lips. Reluctantly, Donnie took his tray back to the kitchen.

"Don't go anywhere. I will be back for you real quick."

He went to the front door and shouted.

"Who is it? Etta Mae's not home!"

"It's Damien!" The voice on the other side of the solid oak four-paneled door responded.

"Damien Whitman. Is this the Smith's home?"

The name Damien was all Donnie heard.

"O' Lord, it's the devil himself! Here we go."

He had just watched *The Omen* on Monday night. The 1976 classic of an American ambassador who learned to his horror, his son was the literal Antichrist.

Donnie grabbed at his chest. His heart raced a mile a minute.

"O, Lord, The old soul-snatcher has come for me! Etta Mae I'm going. Good bye honey."

The knocking and doorbell ringing persisted. The vigilant fly had flown in and watched from its perch on the back of the leather recliner.

"First, it was that animal skinned wearing incarnated ghost and now him! What am I going to do?" The frightened man lamented.

"Wait! I can't go yet . . . at least not with him."

This was a frightening situation. Donnie paced to and fro in front of the door.

"Listen, Old Slew Foot, if you're looking for my wife, she's not here."

"Slew Foot?" The perplexed visitor shouted.

The visitor was at a loss in what exactly was happening on the other side of the door.

"Listen man, I'm not looking for Etta Mae, but I am looking for . . ."

"Then, uh, surely you're not looking for me. I don't have any dealings with you. I went to church last Sunday, and I'm definitely going tomorrow!"

"Dude! What are you rambling about?"

Damien couldn't believe what he had just heard. He placed both hands on either side of the doorpost and leaned in with his face only inches away.

"I'm not looking for Etta Mae, nor you for that matter, but I am looking for my wife!"

"Your wife . . . you have a wife?"

"Are you going to let me in and stop all this crazy bull or what?"

"No! You can't come in here. I plead the blood of Jesus! You can't have my soul. Satan, get thee behind me, or at least get under my feet."

The weak spot on the wood floor creaked as the nervous man paced. The creaking only added to the freaky dilemma he found himself in.

"Etta Mae! Where are you? I need you now!"

"You need who now?"

The heated visitor looked threateningly toward the door and asked another question.

"And why are you calling me Satan?"

"Well, I-I just naturally assumed . . ."

"Brotha, you know what they say about assuming. But, believe me, I just come for my wife and that's all."

On the inside of the door, a recollection of sorts suddenly took place.

"That's right his wife, Dee! Oh man!"

Donnie gave his forehead an open handed smack.

"How stupid of me, this must be Dee's current husband, but was his name . . . Damien? I-I can't remember."

Donnie wiped the sweat from his brow and began to compose himself. The effects of the morning's encounter had apparently been more traumatic than he had first realized.

"Whew! Thank God! But you just cannot keep up with that woman's men folk."

Donnie finally swung the front door open with a sheepish grin plastered on his face.

"Yo! C-can I help you?"

At that exact time, the same mysterious fly chose to conveniently exit the premises.

The loud buzzing sound of its beating wings caused the two men to duck and dodge.

Damien Whitman, a tall trimmed specimen of a man with lines of neat and pleasing symmetry stood at the door. He was dressed in a crisp casual beige linen shirt opened at the collar.

The long lean legs were housed in the finest linen slacks that topped the tan Testoni Norvese leather loafers.

The gold Rolex watch caught the light of the afternoon sun and sent a blinding flash into Donnie's eyes.

The dapper gentleman pushed past the peculiar host. His eyes ran to and fro as he frantically called his wife's name.

"Delilah, Delilah!"

"Hold up dude, slow your roll!" Donnie cautioned.

"Man back up off me!" The highly miffed intruder barked. "Where is she, where's my wife?"

He stared menacingly at the equally perturbed homeowner and shouted once again.

"I said where is my wife? I know she's here!"

"Whoa, there Bro, you don't know jack!"

Donnie was prepared to block any blow he thought might come his way.

"Damn it! Your wife ain't here and you can't just waltz up in my house like a linebacker out of hell!"

"Okay . . . I'm sorry dude, and I apologize, but this is the home of Etta Mae Smith isn't it?"

"Yes, it is." Donnie said. "But it isn't exactly my day to keep up with your wife. Heck, I can't even keep up with my own let alone yours."

"I'm sorry, and I should've known better, but this so damn frustrating." Damien said.

"Now, let me get this straight. My wife's sister, Dee is your wife."

"Dee? Delilah, Delilah Whitman you mean?" Damien corrected.

"And exactly what do you want with Dee?"

"I-I'm not going to hurt her if that's what you're asking. I just don't know where else she could've gone. She just left so fast."

"I wonder why?" Donnie said under his breath.

"What was that?" Damien harshly inquired.

"Nothing at all Brotha-Man."

"I came home to discover she'd packed her bags and had taken off. I figured she'd come here. Delilah always talked about her big sister Etta Mae."

"How did you get my address and know how to find this house?"

"I looked in my wife's Rolodex. Then I rented a car at the air port with a GPS and it brought me right to your door."

"And here you are at my door." Donnie said.

"Come to think of it, perhaps Delilah just hasn't arrived here yet. But I know she's bound to at sometime or other."

Somewhat disappointed the perplexed gentleman turned to leave.

Donnie felt a tinge of empathy for the distressed man's plight. He hoped his next words would offer some ray of hope.

"She's here, but she's not here."

"What exactly are you saying, dude?" Damien asked.

"Your wife was here."

"Would you please just spell it out already?"

"I mean she arrived here late yesterday. But don't ask me where she is now." Donnie threw up both his hands.

"You're saying she's here but you don't know where she is? Now how foolish is that?"

"Look, all I know is she left a short time after my wife. She got up from her nap and said she wanted some fresh air. After she showered, off she went."

This news irritated the deserted husband even more. He began to pace the floor.

"Once again, she just up and leaves. That seems to be her thing lately. She didn't even tell me she was gone."

"To set your mind at ease, I don't think she's gone too far. She didn't leave with a suitcase or anything."

"And you know women and their shoes, and believe me she won't get too far with the type shoes she had on."

"Good!" Then that means she's coming back."

This bit of information appeared to have soothed the savage beast. Damien talked more to himself than to his host.

"I've got to explain . . . and she'll accept my explanation. Yes, she just has to!"

"Oh, she does, aye? Let me ask you something, 'Bubba' . . . Do you think you can?"

"Oh? Why'd you say that?"

"Think about it. Would you if the shoe were on the other foot?"

Damien was at a loss for words. It just could be that he was expecting too much from his wife after what he'd put her though. But, yet, he could still hope.

"You said you flew in this morning, what took you so long to get here?"

"I had time to sit and think. So I booked a hotel room instead of jumping back on the plane. I almost decided to wash my hands of the whole matter."

"Well, okay then, nothing like being truthful." Donnie's mind drifted back to the visitor's name.

"To tell you the truth, Damien, you had me scared for a moment, when you said you were Damien."

He had to chuckle at the thought himself. Donnie then went on to explain why he had delayed opening the door.

"I thought you were s-someone else. You know what I mean?"

"What . . . Oo-oh! Now I get it. Y-you mean you were expecting my boy Lucifer? Man, that's dope!" Damien laughed.

"Hey, you never know!" Believe me when I tell you . . . after what I've seen today; anything can happen up in here!"

"I sure don't know what's been happening to you, but like you, people do joke about me being the devil. Or, they'd ask if my Mom was into voodoo, or some stupid shit like that."

"No, I wouldn't particularly be too proud to be called Damien. How did you feel about having that name?"

"I live with it, that's what I do."

"Have you seen *The Omen,* that 70's movie? Wait a minute, on second thought, exactly how old are you?"

"Dude, what does my age have to do with some damn movie?" The frustrated man walked away.

"I just thought I'd ask."

"If you must know, I'm thirty-nine.

"I just thought you may have been too young to know what I was talking about, the reason I asked."

"Humph, I highly doubt it."

"The Omen then is about this young boy who was possessed . . . never mind. Un-less, you watched it on Monday night."

"No, I didn't watch anything on Monday night. Look, could we just get off my name. I've lived with it this long, and I'll continue to live with it so . . . ."

"Now, you do know what your name means don't you?"

Donnie could not miss an opportunity to show his expert opinion in obsolete topics

"Nope, I hadn't given it any thought whatsoever. But, I'm sure the walking encyclopedia is about to tell me!"

"Well . . . Damien is a boy's name, but get this, it can also be used as a girl's too."

Donnie hid a snicker behind his hand.

"And your point is?" Damien asked with a raised brow.

"Oh, nothing just that it comes from the Greek and it means "to tame, to subdue.

Now you're going to love this one. The Greek root of Damien can also mean spirit or something close to it."

"Would you please cut it out? Man . . . damn!"

"Okay, homie . . . . sorry."

Donnie stepped around the houseguest and settled on the couch.

"Listen! I don't know what to tell you. All I know is I can't even explain what's been going on in my house, let alone your situation! Ghosts popping out of the woodwork and . . ."

"What? What ghost?"

The casual remark had caught the wayfaring visitor off guard.

Donnie was pleased. He had meant for his statement to be a distraction. A well timed ploy had often served as a great coping method for many of his golfing buddies' marital dilemmas.

"Your house haunted or something, dude?"

Damien looked around the room as if seeing it for the first time.

"What house isn't haunted?" Donnie said. "Unless you built it from the ground up, you never know who died in it."

"Believe me, I for damn sure would know." Damien said.

"There is a law that says a seller has to disclose it if a death had occurred in a home before it's purchased."

"Oh, is that right?"

"But still, even then you couldn't be sure . . . the home could have been built over an old cemetery, you never know."

"As much as I hate to say it, you could be right."

Damien remembered the movie *Poltergeist* he had seen as a young boy.

"No wonder you thought I was the devil!" He jumped toward Donnie and shouted. "Boo!"

"Ohh! Fool, don't do that to me!"

"Sorry, but I couldn't resist. And the look on your face was priceless!"

"Well I'm still not convinced you're not!" Donnie emphatically stated.

"Well, I'm not! And as far as that goes, you're the one who's seeing ghosts!"

"Okay, okay, you got me there, 'Brotha-Man." Donnie said, relenting. "I don't know what to make of it."

"Believe me when I tell you. If it was me, I would definitely know!"

"Well . . . all I know is that I went to take a shower, when I heard a voice other than my wife's and Tonika's.

So, when I came down the hall to investigate, the two women were having hissy fits."

"Tonika, now who is she? And where was Delilah?"

"Tonika's my wife's best friend. Our neighbor from across the street, or I should say, the pest from across the street."

"Look man, this is some scary you know what, going on up in here. And you did look as if you'd seen a ghost when I came in.

"I'm not ashamed to admit it. I've really been frightened today."

"And what was up with your friend, the fly?"

"The heck if I know! At least he flew out. Dang it . . . I sure hope the bastard didn't land his butt on my sandwich!"

"You can bet on it. That's what flies do you know." Damien jokingly said.

"Oh crap! Along with you, he had to pop up. I betch'a he ruined my dang sandwich!"

"Sorry, my bad." Damien said.

"Course now, in these days and times everything's popping up . . . and coming out. Gays and ghosts! Flies, and . . . gays." Donnie said, smirking.

"Man!" Damien huffed. He'd chosen to ignore the gaunt chap's last remark.

"I don't know if I want to be here with you. So just give me my wife and I'm out 'a here!"

"Shucks, it's getting to the point I'm almost afraid to be in my own home."

The two men skeptically surveyed the room.

"Etta-a Mae . . . Come home!"

"*Ha, ha, ha*! What's a big boy like you doing being afraid of a little ole ghost?" Damien found the man's fearful demeanor hilarious.

"Boo!" He shouted once again.

"Yo Bro,' what's up with that fear you have going there?"

Damien covered his mouth to hide a grin.

"Say . . . I wouldn't be laughing if I were you, because you're surely in for a rude awakening. And from what I hear, you sure could use a little awakening."

Donnie walked into the dining area. He had missed lunch and wanted to check on his sandwich that was sure to be stale.

"Rude awakening?"

Damien asked as he followed closely on the retreating man's heels. Donnie abruptly stopped and the two collided.

"Damn, are you smoking weed or something?" Damien asked as he backed off. "What does my being awaken have to do with anything?"

"Oh, it's nothing dude."

Donnie knew they could go on for hours berating each other. He turned to face his house guest and extended his right hand for a handshake.

"Tell you what partner, enough with all this crazy talk. Let's just start all over . . . okay?"

"You're on!" Damien shook the extended hand of truce.

Chapter Thirteen

"A compost heap Tonika, really?" Etta Mae said as her eyes followed her friend's gaze. They nonchalantly waved to the approaching figure.

"I must say you do have a way with words."

"Well I would like to think so."

"Ashad really is growing like a weed though. When I saw him and Josh on Tuesday he looked so tall and gangly." Etta Mae said.

Tonika stifled the sob that rose up from the recesses of her soul. The thought of knowing the close relationship Ashad had with Josh had possibly ended was too much for her to reckon with.

Stephanie Willis eagerly greeted the two ladies with outstretched arms.

The flamboyant chatty-Kathy talked rapidly in run-on sentences. The two ladies had realized early on just how pointless it would be to get a word in edgewise with her.

"Hey Sistah-Girls! What's been up with ya, how've you been?"

"We're good." Tonika managed to say.

Stephanie's slender frame was softly draped in a paisley purple and lavender ruffled tank dress that rose mid-thigh. Small ear lobes were burdened with heavy Silverstone owl earrings that hung just below the well-defined jaw line.

Stephanie seemingly appeared to tower some six inches taller than her usual five-foot-five stature. This was all done with the help of the pretty, purple, peep-toe Prata six inch heels.

"Etta Mae did you drive that fine new car of yours or are you boycotting the gas pumps too?"

"No, we . . ."

"Oh, I see it, so never mind. How does it ride? Tonika, girl you love riding in that fine ride don't ya?"

"It rides smooth enough but I . . ."

"Umph, can I say I left my car in my garage?" Stephanie continued on. "I certainly won't about to drive that old gas-aholic not with the bus driving right past my apartment too!"

The neighbors exchanged knowing glances.

"People, I swear! It just does not make any sense with gas prices being at $5.00 a gallon."

Etta Mae and Tonika shifted their feet and patiently waited.

"There just ought to be a law. Can you believe it?"

Tonika, hoping to slow the flow hurriedly interrupted Stephanie's over exuberant chatter.

"Girl, I love those shoes you have on. And you got 'em from FSP didn't you?"

"Now how'd you guess? Yes girl they're from the Fabulous Shoe Palace, because they're so fabulous!"

Etta Mae hid a smirk by turning her head.

"You guys going to the shoe sale? I'm telling you, honey, I hit those sales like a ball hitting a bat. Uh, I meant, a bat hitting a ball . . . well, you know what I mean."

"Yeah, we know exactly what you mean. You were on that sale like spots on a cheetah." Etta Mae said.

"I know that's right." Tonika added.

"Boy, it sure is warm out here."

Stephanie frantically fanned her face with both hands.

"Yes it is, and we should be getting out of this heat." Etta Mae declared, taking a step forward to do just that.

Just as they were about to make their way to the mall's entrance, the driver of a Black LS 460 Lexus honked and waved to the three companions. The car's driver was a Mrs. Porter, a well-to-do philanthropist from the Hampkins.

Stephanie hesitantly returned the wave. She couldn't help but share a bit of gossip with the girls as she watched the luxury sedan weave its way through the parking lot.

"O, Lord, now will you look at that. Humph, Mizz *Porter*. Now ain't she something? Driving around like she's Mizz *Goldfinger*. She needs to go into that big crib of hers and not come out."

"You would say that Miss Coveting Cora. From where I'm standing, it looked to me as if she was friendly enough to you." Etta Mae stated. "I just happen to think the woman is rather nice."

"Uh, huh, if you say so." Stephanie interjected.

"Well, now I'm just saying, that's how it looked to me." Etta Mae added. "So think what you want. Plus, she didn't have to wave at your trifling butt, you know."

"Yeah, she's nice in her own way." Tonika added. "You just have to get to know her. Besides, she can't help it if she's been super blessed. We should all be so lucky."

"Girl, sounds like you've had the distinct pleasure of meeting her." Stephanie said.

"Yep, I have! And it just so happens that she's my soror, so back up off my sistah!"

"I never knew that." Etta Mae said, astonished. "Girlfriend I swear, you never cease to amaze me."

"Remind me to talk to you about it later, okay?" Tonika said.

"Yes, we certainly must talk. Etta Mae said."

"Ah-umf, well, I'm glad for your upcoming talking appointment, but I do hope you know looks can be deceiving." Stephanie was all too eager to divulge the latest rumor. She leaned in and whispered.

"You haven't heard the latest on your girl now have you?"

"No, I haven't heard anything. Have you Tonika?"

"No, not lately . . . So what's ole Miss P. supposedly done now?"

"Well . . ." Stephanie began. Now that she had their attention the rumormonger proceeded to share the latest gossip she'd acquired.

"My Bobbie told me she tried to corner her landscaper into going to bed with her."

"Shut up! You're lying." Tonika shouted. "She did what?"

"Now why would she do that?" Etta Mae gave Stephanie a disapproving look. "Now why would a high society dame like her do something so callous?"

"I do not believe that." Tonika said. "Stephanie is just trying to start something. Besides, that woman has a husband."

"She sure does." Etta Mae added.

"And not only a husband, but a pretty damn rich one at that. Now run and tell that!" Tonika snapped her fingers in Stephanie's face.

"So what, since when has being married ever stopped the red rooster from knocking up the neighbor's prized hens? Aye, To-ni-ka?"

"W-wha-at?" Tonika gasped.

"Ummph, they said the old girl called Josiah into her mansion by pretending her petunias were wilting.

They say she snuck up behind my man Joe, and grabbed him.

But, all she got was coat because they say boyfriend shot out of there so fast.

I don't blame him though, because I know he does not, I repeat, does not want to tackle the Porter dude." Stephanie's guttural laughter rang through the parking lot.

Etta Mae couldn't help but find the humor in the storytelling, but the humor was lost on her befuddled colleague. The insinuated remark made earlier was still echoing in her mind.

Exactly what did Stephanie mean by saying that? Does she know something I should know?

Tonika inquiringly searched the talebearer's eyes, only to receive a mere wink followed with a silently mouthed, call me.

"Here, let me give you my cell number."

Tonika immediately fished around in her purse and came up with a pen.

Etta Mae looked questionably from one to the other, but neither offered any explanation.

Stephanie picked up where she'd left off with Mrs. Porter.

Now they say Mr. P. got connections, and I'm not just talking business connections either. If you know what I mean; rat-a-tat-tat-tat!"

"Mr. Porter is gone a lot." Tonika added. "He's always traveling. I hope they're business trips."

In a barely audible breath, she added. "I guess the poor girl does get lonesome."

The conversation was beginning to hit too close to home, so with a feigned cheerfulness, Tonika exclaimed.

"Plus, you know what they say; "when the cat's away, the mouse will . . .

"Pla-ay . . . he-ey!"

They all finished the sentence. This called for a round of high five between the three acquaintances. Etta Mae, unfortunately, had to jump to reach their highly extended hands.

"Now, you two know you're wrong. How're you going to make me jump like that? But Stephanie, girl your story reminds me of something similar."

"It does . . . something like what?"

"It reminds me of . . ."

"Shucks, that's no excuse just because the man travels." Stephanie suddenly said.

"Minds you of what, Etta Mae?"

Tonika asked.

"He has to keep a roof over that coiffure head. My girl's hair is never out of place." Stephanie continued, not missing a beat.

"Honey not only a roof but you saw the car she was driving. And you see she certainly wasn't trying to save any gas." Tonika added. She and Stephanie touched fists and laughed.

"Yes, and did you two haters notice what her custom tags read?"

"DON'T H-8-T . . . Don't hate! So don't hate you two."

"Etta Mae, girl, you're standing in a parking lot just like us. So why are you tripping?"

"You're right, I am standing in the parking lot, but I'm trying to go into the mall. And I am certainly not hating. Or better yet, I'm not coveting that Lexus either."

"And neither are we!" Tonika said, just as pointedly. "But we were just making an observation."

"Ah, heck, that's why snooty people drive those old damn elite machines anyways." Stephanie added. "Just so they can front and others can gawk."

"Now, you're right about that." Tonika agreed. "It's like they're all saying; "look at what I've got, don't you wish it was yours?"

"That may very well be true, but all I'm saying is material things and luxuries of this world are only temporary." Etta Mae said to drive her point home.

"Tonika, now you do know where I'm going with this don't 'cha?"

"Uh-Oh, here we go." Tonika jokingly said to Stephanie.

"Let me guess . . . could it be the Bible?" She threw up her hands in surrender.

"I swear, Etta Mae and her living WORD. Stephanie, this woman is the only one I know that can bring that book to life. And I mean literally bring it to life."

"Where are you going with this, Etta Mae?" Stephanie inquired. "You keep mentioning . . ."

Tonika playfully grabbed Stephanie by the arm.

"Girl, I'm warning you!"

"What?"

The phenomenon virgin thought the women were merely joking, and had begun to laugh.

"That's right they do call it *the* Living Word, don't they?"

The complex conversation had become a bit too disturbing to the baffled woman, so Tonika felt the need to recount their morning's escapade.

"We're not joking honey. We had a ghostly visitation just this morning. We were visited by the first lady herself."

"Stop lying girl!" The paranormal skeptic bowled over with laughter once again. "Michelle Obama ain't been to your house!" Y'all are some fools!"

"No dunce! I'm talking about the very *first* woman; Eve. Whenever my friend here begins to talk Bible . . . well you just wait."

"Wait for what, and did you say Eve like Adam's Eve? The apple biter?"

"Uh-huh, but it 'probly wasn't an apple."

"You mean to tell me a ghost visited you two, and what do you mean it wasn't an apple?"

"Yep, that's what we're saying exactly." Etta Mae said.

"Damn! Now I know y'all's crazy."

"Well . . . chick-a-dee, I wouldn't call us crazy because it really did happen." Tonika said.

"At whose house did you say? Stephanie inquired. "I want to know so I can make sure I don't take my black butt over there."

"But if you think about it Stephanie, it's not that unusual." Tonika said. "The spirit realm is all around us even now."

"Well, if you say so, Tonika. Anything is possible, I-I guess."

Understandably, Stephanie was still not convinced, so Tonika tried another ploy.

"Think about it! Paranormal activity is accepted as a common occurrence now. What's preventing anything from coming through opened portals?"

"Stop playing fool, this crap you're talking is not funny." Stephanie adamantly stated. "I haven't called up *no-body*, and I don't want to see no-body. Understand?"

"Well, I didn't exactly call up any-body either, but she came." Tonika said.

Stephanie mulled the context of the conversation over in her mind.

"You know, Mrs. Porter's dilemma reminds me of the story of Joseph."

"Who?" Stephanie and Tonika asked jointly.

"Joseph! You know, Israel's son.

Abraham, Isaac, and Jacob remember?"

Etta Mae looked at the two women expectedly, but blank stares were all she received.

"The Old Testament in the book of Genesis." She got nothing.

"I swear you two! Joseph was a young boy whose idiot brothers had sold him to a traveling band of Ishmaelite all because of jealousy. Now do you remember?"

"O, yeah!" Tonika winked at Stephanie. "Now, I remember. In fact I was just reading about it the other night."

"I'm sure you were Tonika." Etta Mae knowingly joked.

"I'm not lying, Etta Mae! You said Genesis, right? It's just that maybe I didn't get as far as I would've cared to but . . ."

The look on Etta Mae's face alerted Tonika that her explanation was pointless.

"I know you don't believe me, but go ahead, you're going to tell us about it anyways." She turned to Stephanie and said.

"You'd better listen closely to what you hear, because believe me, you will see it again."

"Well . . ." Etta Mae began. "As the story goes, it seemed that Potiphar, the Pharaoh's right hand man had a wife like Mrs. Porter. Who had everything she'd wanted, except the attention of her husband, you understand. She'd lie around all day just watching poor Joseph as he went about his daily duties. Just drooling and lusting after him."

"Loungers always seem to get in trouble. You know what they say; "An idle mind certainly is the devil's workshop." Stephanie added.

"Yes, you could say that but in the old girl's defense, Joseph was good on the eyes, and he was exceptionally good at what he did. Do you feel me?"

"We feel you. Right, Stephanie?"

Stephanie had been distracted by a familiar white Cordova whose driver she recognized.

"Huh, what did you say?"

She turned her attention once again to the street and waved to some co-workers going by.

"She's not listening, that girl's mind is about as long as that scalped hair-do she's sporting." Etta Mae snapped her fingers in the clueless face. "Stephanie, stay with us!"

"Etta Mae stop it!" Tonika said laughing. "When did you become so devious?"

"Well, it's true!"

"Oh! You were saying something about a Joseph." Stephanie said.

"I was saying, my man Joe ran the place, while Potiphar was off doing his thing. And can I tell you, Potiphar trusted Joseph with everything? That is everything except his wife."

They all broke into hysterics.

"Well . . . One day Sistah-Girl got Joseph in so much trouble, and all because she couldn't control herself."

"You know what y'all? It is sure enough hot as you know what out here." Stephanie said. "I'm dying to hear the outcome of your story, but why don't we just finish this little tale inside the mall where it's cooler. Okay? Anyhow, I'll have to catch the next bus."

She picked up her bags and headed toward the mall entrance without bothering to see if the ladies were following. They were of course.

A blast of cold air engulfed them with a welcoming relief when the automatic doors opened.

The women quickly made their way to the nearest bench as their tired feet were yelling for the much needed reprieve.

"Whew! That's much better." Stephanie said.

The mall was surprisingly empty for a Saturday evening. It looked almost as if they'd walked into a twilight zone, as was the name of the mall."

"I don't get it, the parking lot is full, but where are all the people?" Stephanie said.

The Look of Love is in your eyes . . . . suddenly began to play over the air waves."

The song had a hypnotic effect on the women. Their eyes closed and they swayed in unison to the melodious tune.

"*O' my God!* Y'all, look!" Stephanie yelled.

Something most unusual had happened. An incarnated apparition stood before them.

"Uh, ladies, this is so w-weird."

"O, no!" Tonika yelled. "They're following us, Etta Mae! We can't escape 'em!"

"Who's following you?" Stephanie asked. "And why is she dressed like Mark Anthony's Cleopatra?"

"That, my friend, apparently is Mrs. Potiphar." Etta Mae remarked.

"Miss Who?" Stephanie reached for her bags. "Are you fools crazy? Ghosts have been visiting you all day, and you two act like its normal!"

"What else can we do?" Etta Mae asked.

"I don't know, but I'm getting out of here and away from you two."

"Now just hold on."

Etta Mae threw out her arm to restrain Stephanie's flight.

"It's all good, they're harmless enough. At least this way you're getting to hear the Bible first hand."

"You sure are." Tonika added. "This is the Bible, walking and talking."

"Mrs. Potiphar was a sight to behold as an Egyptian royalty. The transposed figure was dressed in a gold satin body-hugging, floor length gown that ended in at least a foot of train.

A bejeweled serpent head-dress adorned the braided jet black hair. Eyelids embellished with dark shades of purple dramatized a flawless oval face.

The fixed piercing eyes were lined with the thickest of black char-coal.

The finely chiseled nose with narrowed nostrils sat above pouting lips, seemingly as ripe, and as swollen as a newly picked pomegranate. Elongated ornate gold pear shaped earrings, ending in small blossoms of flowers dangled from delicate pierced ears.

The three mesmerized women nervously watched as she approached them.

"Humph" She uttered, in a raspy seductive voice. *"I don't know what Joseph was talking about, but I know I had it going on. When he thought I wasn't looking, I caught him watching me out of the corner of his eye. He pretended he wasn't interested in what I had to offer, but, as you can see, I knew better."*

Beautiful hands slid seductively over a curvaceous figure.

"After all, who could keep their eyes off of all this? And besides . . . I'm working this dress."

"Oh, no she didn't!" Stephanie defiantly said. "Did you all hear that? "Who could keep their eyes off all this?" Now ain't she something?"

"I take it women were full of themselves even back then." Tonika said.

"Ladies, don't try to comprehend it all just yet. Just listen and learn . . . listen and learn." Etta Mae said.

The swishing sound made by the elaborate gown every time she moved was the only sound heard in the mall's corridor.

"Well . . . if you all are finished."

The three chatty observers became motionless. Mrs. Potiphar started in on her saga once again.

"Thank you! . . . Now as it turns out old Joseph could."

"I'm sorry, but I forgot what you had said before." Tonika said.

"Keep his hands off of all that." Etta Mae reminded her. Mrs. Potiphar waited patiently with hands on her hips.

"You see it went something like this. My plan was to take our master/ servant relationship a little further. I'd given the household servants the day off, and called Joseph into the house. Then I proceeded to put the squeeze on him. I grab him, but all it got me was a hand full of coat!"

"Now I know who you are." Stephanie declared. "All those years in Sunday School as a child have finally paid off. But I have one question to ask you."

"You have a question for me?"

"Yes mam."

"Well, pray tell. What is your question?"

"Why were you grabbing all up on that man? And it certainly wasn't your prerogative because Women's Lib was nowhere to be found then. Now am I right ladies?"

"You're right." Etta Mae agreed.

"You got that right. That's what we call sexual harassment in these days and times." Tonika said.

"Why do you think in deed? If you ask me, the whole fiasco has been over played. It wasn't enough I was made to feel inferior in my day, but now I have to endure it today."

"I don't know why you would say something like that. We're talking about a man's life." Etta Mae said. "How do you justify your actions?"

"How? Do you really want to know?"

"Yes!" They all shouted.

"*Simply because there's no doubt in my mind female slaves were made available for my husband, so I just figured a male slave should've been available for me.*"

"Oh, you did, did you?" Tonika said.

"*Oh, and did I mention he was easy on the eyes? And the fact that my husband was seemingly always gone didn't help any.*"

"So what you're basically saying is that your husband was gone a lot, but he wasn't really gone?"

Stephanie addressed Mrs. Potiphar with eyes narrowed.

"And if I understand you correctly, Joseph supposedly got into all that trouble because your love muffin was missing in action too often?"

"*My love muffin . . . what's this muffin thing?*"

"Potiphar, your husband dear, and poor Joseph, the poor thing didn't see the light of day for years." Etta Mae said.

"*Well if that's what you read, but none of it was my fault.*"

Stephanie's spirit rose up in anger behind the snug smirk on Mrs. Potiphar's face.

"Now ain't that a blip! Well, whose fault was it then?"

She felt the need to defend Joseph's honor against the arrogant spirit.

"It sure wasn't Joseph's. It wasn't his fault Mr. P couldn't take care of business."

"You go girl! You're on a roll." Tonika said encouragingly. Etta Mae looked on in total silence.

"Oh, that's nothing." Tonika intervened. "That crap still happens today. I know you heard about the man who surprised his wife and her lover in a truck.

The woman realized she'd been caught red handed cried rape. The husband shot the dude. Bang! Killed 'im dead. And that wasn't too long ago either. You remember that Etta Mae?"

Etta Mae shook her head in acknowledgement.

"Ladies please!" Give me a break. It's not as if it was something I did all the time!"

The women fell silent once again, startled at the sudden outburst.

"It was . . . well it was just that Joseph was such a fine specimen of a man; handsome, intelligent, shrewd, and a born leader. Not to mention having his God's favor."

Etta Mae's head shook in agreement, along with Stephanie and Tonika.

"You may be right about that, but go on tell your story." Etta Mae said.

"There he was day in and day out, with rippling muscles, always there for me to see. I bet it would've been hard for even you three not to have been enticed. You do know that Mother Nature's raging fires burn brightly on her own don't you?"

"Yes, they do, but we have our own fireman to put out our fires. Well . . . at least I do." Etta Mae said.

Pleased with themselves on Etta Mae's comeback, the ladies slapped high fives.

"What are you three imbeciles saying? In case you didn't know it, my slaves were there to do my every bid. When I clapped my hands, they jumped. And dare I say how high. I'm not used to being denied anything!"

"There, there, easy now Miss P., don't go getting your panties in a bunch. We didn't mean to upset . . ."

"Panties in a bunch!" Stephanie was overcome with laughter once again.

"Now that's a good one. The question is, did she even wear panties?"

Etta Mae and Tonika merely chuckled.

The Egyptian specter didn't know what to make of such a barbaric display of humor. Surely these women understood her plight.

Didn't that one with the tight ponytail just make a reference to the same thing happening to someone a few days ago? Why then do they find my tale so overwhelming?

"You ladies just don't seem to understand. Joseph wouldn't submit to me, a-and I just lost it. That man was so sure of himself!"

"Sistah-Girl." Etta Mae had had enough. "What you didn't know was that Joseph was only being true to his God, as well as showing his gratitude to your husband. And besides, you knew for yourself that Joseph had the run of the place. So, don't even trip."

"So tell me Miss Lust Bunny, what did Joseph do after you cornered him?" Stephanie said.

"What do you think he did? You supposedly read the story in what you call your Sunday School."

Not one to back down from a confrontation, Mrs. Potiphar went toe to toe with the cropped-hair tyrant.

"I told you, he took off like a bat out of hell, leaving coat behind and ego too."

"And if I remember correctly that's when you framed him you old Jezebel." I swear I feel about you, just about how I feel about that Eve." Tonika said.

"Who are you calling a Jezebel? You don't know me. You may think you do, but you do not."

"Oh, don't worry yourself too much, honey." Etta Mae pointedly stated. "But you do bear a striking resemblance in character to old Jezzie though. You're both conniving."

Now, I don't mind talking with this shorter one. She carries herself much better than the other two. A passive demeanor is much more pleasing than an aggressive one. Mental note to self; take a chill pill every once and awhile."

She proceeded to answer the posed question.

"To answer your question . . . it was just that I got to thinking. I didn't want to mess up what I'd had . . . I mean, I did have all the luxuries and trappings a woman could want. So I figured I had better protect myself just in case Joseph decided he'd wanted to squeal."

She addressed this to Etta Mae, more so than to the others.

"I couldn't have that. Joseph was such a loyal and faithful servant to his master, so I beat him to the punch. After all, I still had his coat as proof. So, when as you say, Mr. P. got home, I told him his best servant, his most loyal Hebrew slave had tried to seduce me."

"Just lied through your teeth!" Stephanie shouted. "And I bet ya weren't a bit ashamed. Were you?"

"Nope, I can't say I was. Honey, I was saving my own neck. Plus, I needed to show Joseph you don't deny Mrs. Potiphar anything and get away with it."

And Potiphar, just like a big dummy fell for your lie?" Stephanie asked.

"Hook, line and sinker, as you say. The man was livid to say the least. "To the dungeon with you!" He had yelled. "The dungeon? So I thought . . . now wait a minute that was supposed to cost that man his head.

She stepped away, with head lowered.

"But what it really told me was that my husband actually believed in his slave more than he did me."

"Aha! So it turned out he wasn't as dumb as you thought."

Tonika couldn't help but comment after listening quietly for a change.

"Apparently not. It seemed he couldn't kill a man he knew in his heart was innocent. But due to his reputation and pride, he had to punish the once valued slave in some way. And as fate would have it,

Joseph, as you know became even greater in prison, interpreting dreams and all."

"Yay, way to go Joe!" Stephanie exclaimed. Tonika and Etta Mae also clapped and cheered on the slave's behalf.

"Yaa-aay! I for one am just glad your husband saw through your big lie and didn't hurt that poor innocent man." Tonika said.

"Miss P you couldn't have known it at the time, but God was going to use Joseph in a mighty way. And Joseph said it himself, and I paraphrase, "What the devil meant for bad, God used it for His good to save many lives."

And another thing, it wasn't Pot's doing either. It was divine providence. Joseph was going to save those brothers of his, along with a whole nation. The PP & B were just humbling assignments for God's servant, that's all. So don't go beating yourself up about it too much, okay."

"You think so Etta Mae. But what's this PP & B?"

"I'm sorry, but PP&B stands for the pit, the palace, and the brothers. Oh, and I forgot one, the prison."

"Now, I see . . . I didn't know."

The grand dame had been truly touched by her favorite human's words. Unlike the other two she devils, the kind woman had cared enough to extend the olive branch.

"Well, that makes me feel better, but ladies things were never the same between my husband and me after that. He never trusted me again."

"Boo, hoo, hoo what a shame, and after all you went through."

Mrs. Potiphar turned to personally address the antagonizing being.

"Stephanie, I believe? Has anyone ever lost their trust in you?"

"No, I can't think of anyone."

The divorcee was actually in denial about her own marital state, but wasn't about to give this transposed apparition the pleasure of identifying with her plight.

"*No? Or do you choose not to say?*"

Stephanie did not acknowledge the question. The all-knowing spirit allowed the woman's lie to stand.

"*Then you should be so lucky. To tell you the truth, I'm not behind bars so to speak, but I am in a prison, a prison without walls. I'm a prisoner of my own mind, and of my own doing.*"

She turned to walk away, while muttering under her breath.

"*I'm still kicking myself. Good day ladies.*"

Mrs. Potiphar seemingly faded into thin air. The three women sat entranced. Stephanie was the first to speak.

"I don't feel sorry for her. I'm glad her husband handled his business. She didn't need to kick herself." Stephanie shadow kicked the air.

"Boy, I tell you, we sure are some kicking fools today." Etta Mae said. "I feel sorry for the woman, she looked so sad."

The ladies all agreed and discussed it among themselves. Then as if awakening from a dream, they all stared at each other and turned to survey their surroundings.

Familiar sounds once again filled the air. They heard giggling teenagers walking past, a mother scolding her child, and the piano concerto that filled the mall.

"W-what just happened, now that was too spooky?" Stephanie asked in disbelief. She looked to her friends for an explanation.

"Now correct me if I'm wrong, but this mall was empty just a moment ago. A-and we were just talking to a Mizz Poti-phar, right?"

"Yes, that is correct; I warned you in the parking lot." Tonika said.

"You know what, I'm out of here."

Stephanie reached down and gathered her many bags, and made for the nearest exit. Etta Mae and Tonika stared after her.

"Bye, Stephanie!" The deserted women yelled.

"And we do have to talk!" Tonika yelled. "I'll call you!"

The automatic doors closed with a resounding swish behind the hastily retreating woman, who felt as if she'd been in a time warp. Any future association with the likes of Etta Mae Smith and Tonika Gibbons would be far and in between.

The eerie karma surrounding those two were too supernaturally charged for her taste. Never, in all her thirty something years she had never experienced a phenomenon such as that.

Tonika will just have to find another source of information of her husband's exploits, but it will not be coming from Stephanie Nicole Willis.

Fortunately, her bus rounded the corner just at that time.

Tonika looked longingly after the one source she thought could fill in the gap surrounding who was responsible for turning her world upside down. She turned her attention to Etta Mae who'd been watching her changing demeanor.

Chapter Fourteen

"Sorry dude, but we haven't even been properly introduced. Donnie said. "Hello, I'm Donnie Leroy Smith, Etta Mae's husband."

"And I just barged into your home like a charging bull and didn't even properly introduce myself. So please forgive me."

Damien wiped his hand on a pant leg and extended it for a handshake.

"Hi, I'm Damien Darnell Whitman, but my friends call me Double D."

"Double D, now that wouldn't happen to stand for double-dipping now would it?"

"Double-dipping?" He repeated loudly. "Now why the heck would you say something like that?"

The silly statement irritated Damien so much that he responded by shoving Donnie backwards.

"Easy now, big fellow, you don't want to do that." Donnie steadied himself.

"Dee-Dee!" He said laughing under his breath.

"What is so damn funny?"

"Ah, you are my good man."

"Look dude, I'm alright with whatever you call me. I know who I am, and you can bank on that."

The robust house guest shadow boxed the air. Finally, he dropped his hands to his side and stepped toward Donnie, who by then felt a little intimidated, and backed further into the room.

"I've gotten in a few scrapes behind my name you know, but I'm telling you those very same fools had to back up!"

"I'm sure they did." Donnie quipped.

"You see this scar right here?" Damien pointed to a scar above his brow.

"I got that when I was in college, but you should see the other guy."

"Bro, I'm sure you left your mark alright. What did you do slap him?"

He playfully slapped the air with his hands in an effeminate gesture.

"Stop it now . . . quit it."

"Ha, ha, you're so funny."

"No, you're wrong. I'm not the funny one."

"Let's just say, I had the last laugh after it was over and done, because I represented. You know what I mean?"

"I bet you represented alright. But that's not what I heard." Donnie smirked. "Women, they do talk."

"When I said I represented, I represented, just like I'm about to do right now."

Damien threw sucker punches as he approached the annoying host, who in turn, threw up his arm in defense.

"Okay now dude; you'd better back up and loosen those Speedos."

"Do you want some of this?"

"No dude, I'm just joking with you. And besides, you're right,

I don't know you that well. I was just repeating what I thought I picked up from our wives conversation.

"Oh, so I get it, Delilah's been having diarrhea of the mouth."

Damien looked inquiringly at his host. He finally understood his plight and walked over to the couch and sat down.

"You might say that." Donnie said as he took the seat across from his now solemn guest. Instinct said the two were about to charter dangerous waters.

"Just how much has Delilah told her sister?" Damien asked.

"Well to be frank, Dee hasn't really said that much, not even to Etta Mae, but it was more like what she didn't say."

"Oh, so now you're a psychic on top of being a class ass jerk." Damien said.

"If that's what you want to call it. Look, I have to tell you, your girl's pretty pissed off, okay. So I'm just deducing what I think it is."

"You deduce?"

"As a matter of fact you don't have to be a rocket scientist, to know what you closeted brothers are into these days. You can read any magazine and know what time it is."

Donnie kept silent about the conversation he had earlier with his sister-in-law.

"Oh, so you're up on all the latest, huh? Do explain yourself further please sir."

"Man now listen, when women get to a place where they can't talk about something, then you can take it to the bank that it's something too deep for their psyche to grasp."

"Fool, you're tripping."

"Tripping or not, but needless to say, that's what led to my conclusion." Donnie said.

"I can't believe you, dude."

"You're a brother on the DL. Now, you have to admit . . . that's deep."

"So that's how you came up with it, huh?" Damien stood with one hand cupped beneath his chin. "And in all your deducing you came up with I'm on the DL."

"Yep, that's my story and I'm sticking to it."

"Humph!" Damien muttered.

And I tell you something else! I read about you dudes in Schwarz. Uh, oh… damn, now I'm sounding like my wife." Donnie said.

Damien was reminded of a conversation between him and Delilah.

"I'm sure Delilah read that article too. She commented on it at dinner last Thursday."

"I bet that made your old butt squirm." Donnie laughed.

"Let's just say I'm lucky she didn't see the look on my face. And I might add it also helped that my back was turned."

"I just don't see what's so good about all this deception going on with our people." Donnie said.

"Who's deceiving whom?"

"Are you kidding me?"

"Look, I have to say that I have no regrets."

Damien chose not to acknowledge the disdainful look directed his way, but continued on with his statement.

"Life can get pret-ty boring."

"I feel sorry for you, my dear man." Donnie finally said. "You're wrong and you'll have to speak for yourself on that one."

"Please don't pity me kind sir."

"I'm just glad that crap wasn't going on when I was your age."

"Are you serious?"

"Yes, I'm as serious as a heart attack. You young people are something else these days."

"Dude!" Damien shouted. "What world do you live in?"

"Why, the same one as you of course."

"Don't be so sure." Damien countered. "Maybe it's only because Schwarz didn't have the guts to print anything like that back then. You know there's nothing new under the sun, and you can bank on that."

"Yeah, yeah, if you say so, man." Donnie said. "I don't know about you, but if I wrote a book on the exploits of my life, I'd probably end up with a best seller."

He reclined in the chair and interlocked his hands behind his head.

"No, please allow me to be the first." said Damien. "I should write one starting with my childhood."

"Shucks, who needs to write a book, all you have to do is let a woman get a whiff of your secrets and then it's on!" Donnie said. "The phones would be ringing off the hook, with "Girl, did you hear?""

"And not only that, but by the time they finished adding to it your life could be made into the movie of the week."

Raucous laughter erupted between the two.

"Yeah, and you know they'd have to spice it up and make it even juicier than what it actually was." Damien added.

"Etta Mae and Tonika would have a field day with it. And get this, they would find something in the Bible to relate it to. At least my wife would."

Ding dong.

The sound of the doorbell caused Donnie's muscles to tense. He bolted upright from his reclined position. The thought of who it could be held him motionless.

"Here we go again. Now who could this be?"

He looked to the befuddled house guest but had not really expected an answer.

"Damn! It's Grand Central Station around here today."

Donnie opened the door to find a gangly teenager with dreadlocks standing before him with a container filled with items to sell.

"Good afternoon sir, I'm from GITYO, the Get It Together Youth Organization. I was wondering if you'd be interested in buying an item or items to help support our mission. The mission is to keep youth like myself out of trouble by providing a safe and stable environment. The proceeds help support a summer camp for youth like me."

The young man this read from the embossed card he was holding.

"Man you didn't even bother to breathe while you read all that. I'm impressed." Donnie lightheartedly said. "I know you're nervous, I would be too."

"No sir." The young man answered.

"GITYO, huh? Does that stand for git yo act together?"

"No sir."

"Uh um, okay then, you're a man of few words I see. What you got in there?"

"Candy bars, batteries, carwash chamois . . . and some other stuff."

"And some other stuff." Donnie mocked. "Okay young man, I'll help you out. Let me have two of those chocolate candy bars."

"Yes sir, I mean, thank you."

He handed the young man a five spot. "Keep the change."

The young man stood in anticipation.

"Ah, sir, a-actually, I need another five dollars from you, p-please."

"What? You mean to tell me these candy bars are five dollars apiece?"

Yes sir, t-they are."

The young man nervously adjusted the waste of his pants while he waited for the miser to fish into his pockets for another five spot.

"Here you go. You got me on this one, but not again okay."

"Thank you sir, and have a fantastic day."

"And you do the same."

Donnie closed the door and approached Damien. He held the bars of candy as if they were bars of gold.

"Here, you care for one?"

"Sure, thanks."

They quickly tore into the wrappers and gobbled down the sweet delectable in two bites.

"Oh man that hit the spot. I've good mind to tackle my wife's chicken salad, but I want to see tomorrow."

"Go eat that sandwich you made." Damien said. "I'm sure that big fly left you some."

"As far as I'm concerned, he could've taken it with him."

The men shared a much needed laugh.

"So what do you do in your spare time besides hiding in the house?" Damien asked.

"I'm usually on the range, but I wanted to catch this special episode of a show that is long over." Donnie said.

"Sorry, if I spoiled it for you." Damien said. "I bet you put a lot of value in your golfing, don't ya?"

"Yes, it does mean a lot to me." Donnie admitted.

"Now you see how a man's attention can get away from his home life." Damien said.

"Oh, no you don't. You can't put what you do and what I do in the same category."

"All I'm saying dude is as much time you spend on the golf range . . . can any of the fella's say you're actually at the range?"

"And just what might you be implying?"

"I'm just saying . . ." Damien turned his back to Donnie.

"Believe me when I tell you." Donnie forcibly grabbed the instigator's arm and spun him around.

"I'm where I say I am, and my wife knows it! If nothing else my lucky golf shirt can speak for me."

"Lucky golf shirt? What does a shirt have to do with your wife knowing where you are?"

"Now think about it." Donnie chided. "I'm out there in the hot blazing sun, walking and sweating behind this little white ball. If I came home all showered and smelling fresh, don't you think she would suspect something?"

In his best Etta Mae's voice, "Why do you smell so fresh? I thought you went golfing."

"Okay, okay, I get your point, you're right." Damien said amused.

"Humph, I know I'm right. Those ole hawk-eyes don't miss nothing!"

"You sure know your woman, because her sister . . ."

"She had the nerve to wash my shirt the other day before a big tournament and it pissed me off. Then she and ole motor-mouth had a laugh about it."

"What?" Not the infamous golf shirt." Damien said laughing.

"I'm telling you man, I was as mad as a hornet knocked out of his nest!"

Just thinking about it caused Donnie to pace the floor.

"Say man, you do wash the shirt don't you?" Damien asked wrinkling his nose.

"No, I don't, only after a tournament. All my karma might be washed out of it."

Donnie allowed his mind to reflect on his last golf outing.

"Call me superstitious if you want."

"Oh, I'm sure you and that shirt are pleasant to be around."

Damien held his nose again.

"Yeah, yeah, you're so funny." Donnie said. "Let's get back to why you're here. Let me ask you this, does the name Alma Wallington mean anything to you?"

"Yes, I've heard of her." Damien answered. "She's a black author, and her book's called, *Erica Bags a Fledgling*. Why? It's been years since her fiasco of a marriage came to the forefront."

"Good, then you do know what went down with her."

"What made you bring her up?"

"Oh, no reason other than to say your marriage identifies with hers."

Damien set his mind on the task at hand. He sensed the man across from him really wasn't done with the matter of his life.

"Did you ever stop to think about the situation she found herself in?"

"No, and just what are you getting at?"

Damien fidgeted with one of the two multi-colored Phoenician glass rabbits that sat on the coffee table.

"Am I correct in saying it was a bunch of mess, kind sir?" Donnie inquired in his mock Englishman voice.

"Yes, it was, and I'm sorry to say that mental telepathy of yours has paid off. "Damn it to hell!"

Distraught, Damien rose to his feet and walked away with clench fists stuffed deeply in his pant pockets.

"I did hear that she was coping with it pretty well though."

"She said she didn't intend to be a victim any longer. Perhaps that's what my sissy-n-law is thinking too."

"Don't count on it. I'm not going to give up that easily!"

"And I wouldn't go getting any big ideas either if I were you!"

Donnie said with a smug look on his face. "From the looks of it brother, I think your butt's going to go through the ringer!"

"Anyone ever tell you that with a friend like you who needs an enemy?"

"Say what you want but I know Alma's not alone in this. There're other forsaken women going through the very same hell."

Donnie would not allow himself to fall prey to the discomfort his guest was experiencing.

"You sorry brothers ought a' be ashamed of yourselves!"

"I tell you what amazes me." Damien said.

"And what would that be kind sir?"

"How you are all up in my damn business! And I wish you would quit it with the brothers like you crap! Damn it! You're a brother too in case you haven't noticed!"

"Yes, you're right!" Donnie adamantly responded. And I'm all brotha make no mistake about it! Everything's normal about this! Old Hank serves his purpose well, the way he was meant to."

Donnie glanced down at his lower parts.

"With a woman! Now you can bank on that. Hank is definitely not confused what garage he parks in. Just ask my wife."

"Ask my wife, ask my wife this ask my wife that." Damien muttered under his breath.

Donnie heard but didn't bother to respond to the man's sarcasm.

"And I'm sure your wife has a tale of woes on how Hank can't park in the garage anymore because of oil leaks."

"You're full of bull!"

Damien's remark had finally struck a sore cord with the agitated host.

"Believe me you don't want to go there!"

"Slow your road dude! I was just saying. I am sorry to hear that Delilah is upset. I guess I was just hoping; she could understand that's all."

"Fool, you're asking a lot out of that poor woman." Donnie walked away. "And you hope she understands. Man please!"

"Yes, I said I hope she can understand."

"There ain't that much understanding in the world. It's not like you stepped out with another woman, dude, but you cheated with someone with the same equipment as you."

"Now if that's not a slap in the old girl's face, I don't know what is."

Damien stood there absorbing it all. He wasn't thinking too respectful of this sinister man at the moment.

The irritating Don E. Do-Right's constant reminder of how dire the situation he faced was beginning to fray his nerves.

Who did he think he was anyway? And besides, my father used to say that "we all fall short of the glory . . ." So this dude needs to get off his glory horse and come down to where the brothers walk.

"Hello! Are you with me, or have you traveled elsewhere?" Donnie waved his hands before Damien's eyes.

"In case you didn't know it, it's not okay to cheat with another woman either. For all I know, you could've dipped your stick . . ."

Donnie's gasp almost depleted the air supply in the room. The look of astonishment on the offended man's face made it necessary for Damien to hurriedly change the subject.

"Uh, mm, sounds like you have a great wife, if she is anything like Delilah . . ."

"Don't insult me, I wouldn't dare!" Donnie said in a barely audible tight voice.

"Unlike you wimps, I took my wedding vows very serious when I got married and I still do."

"Sorry partner, I didn't know what I said was going to cause such a stir."

The priest of his domain was not willing to admit that he'd once come close to having a fling some years ago with a clerk at the country club. He recognized that experience as being at his weakest moment.

"Nope, Etta Mae's the only girl for me. And I can't say that the two sisters are anything alike, thank God. More like night and day, oil and water—

"Okay, okay I get the point, geez."

Damien lifted his hands in surrender to curtail the verbal barrage.

"But here's something for you to ponder, maybe you're not replacing her with another woman, but what about that little white ball you run after every chance you get. Huh?"

"I just told you that Etta Mae and Dee are like day and night, and I don't need to be all up under my wife every time she turns around."

"Humph! If you say so, but I'll make it up to Delilah one way or other."

"I don't know man, you'll have to bend over backwards to make this one up!"

Donnie laughed in total abandonment.

"Oops, no pun intended big fella."

"There you go again. You just can't be serious, can you? And why are you so concerned with my sexual exploits?"

"I'm not concerned for my sake, but when it affects what's close to me . . ."

Just then the telephone rang. Donnie lifted the receiver.

"H-hello . . . Oh! Cynthia . . . how're you baby girl? I-we're well. Yes, uh huh . . . well good to hear. Uh huh, I hope you had a fabulous time in the Five-O state. Me and Etta plan to make it over there real soon. Come to think of it, we have an anniversary coming up. Huh? No your sister's not here; she and our neighbor left early today for shopping. You know your sister and her shopping. Ha, ha, ha, ha . . . I know that's right. She did get it honest. O-okay, yeah call her on her cell . . . maybe she'll hear it. Okay, baby, you take care, and we'll be talking with ya soon, okay. Uh huh . . . love you too, bye-bye now."

"That was Cynthia looking for Etta Mae. And you noticed I didn't say anything about you or Dee."

"Yes, I noticed and I don't know whether it was good or bad."

"Well, I figured if you wanted her to know anything, Etta Mae would tell her." The two laughed.

"You know, uh, I mean, I know my wife does love me. Damien interjected. "She knows I'm the best thing that's ever happened to her.

"Do you hear yourself?" Donnie asked.

"Yes I do, plus she's not exactly a spring chicken. Now you do know that. Not to mention that she's been around the block a time or two."

"So . . . what're you doing now? Are you trying to justify why she should take you back, by belittling her?"

"I'm just saying. There are quite a few notches under the old girl's belt. Let's see . . . what am I? Oh yes, number six!"

"Now you see, the moment I start to feel sorry for your bug-ass, you open your mouth and say something dumb.

The woman looks damn good for her age, and I'm sure you didn't turn down any blessings."

Donnie took a stand in his absent sister-in-laws defense.

"It's not like you think. I never said I was a saint; that's your department. But I do have my own money." Damien said.

"I'm sure you do, glad to hear it."

"You see hombre you never know what lies in a man."

Donnie was growing weary by the minute. His favorite program had long since been off the air. He hadn't had a chance to eat his sandwich, and he was still hungry.

"We better be glad those women aren't here to hear all this bull we're shooting!" He said.

Damien stole a look at his watch. "I wonder when Delilah is going to return."

"Ett-aa! Where are you?" Donnie called out.

The strange bed-fellows couldn't help but laugh at the awkwardness of their situation.

"I can't stay here too much longer. I wonder when that woman is coming back." He checked his time piece once again. Donnie watched the man as he nervously fidgeted.

The room was seemingly closing in. Damien undid another button as a trickle of sweat ran down the crevice of his sternum.

Donnie settled down in his Lazy Boy. He felt as if nothing in life was the same anymore. Here he is having this stupid conversation about men on men when all he'd wanted for the evening was a little peace and quiet.

Damien on the other hand oblivious to the thoughts the older gentleman harbored continued with his banter.

"A lot of your sisters are not what they're cracked up to be you know."

"Look, damn it!" Donnie, now beyond being tired, shouted.

He jumped up and crossed the room, and before he knew it, he'd grabbed Damien by the shoulders and attempted to shake him.

"Look! You need to stop with all this crazy chatter. I'm about sick of it."

Damien shook loose of the iron grip, and stepped back. It appeared to him, basically, that the two of them would never see eye to eye on anything.

He had wanted to leave, but hadn't wanted to chance missing his wife's return. But where could neutral ground be found was the question.

Donnie left the room and went into the kitchen. The pang of hunger had become too great to ignore. The forgotten sandwich sat on the counter, beckoning with the look of hunger quenching delight.

"Should I, or shouldn't I? Oh, hell! If it's good enough for that damn fly, then it has to be good enough for me."

He took a knife out of the drawer and divided the super sub in half. He poured two glasses of ice tea and carried the meal back into the living room.

"Aha!" Damien waited with mouthwatering anticipation.

"Sorry about earlier but my stomach was growling, so I broke down and decided my sandwich would become my savior. Care for some?"

"Hell yeah! Let me at it. I was about to drop from hunger myself."

Damien's first thought was about the fly, but his stomach growled, "feed me, feed me" with every passing minute. He reached for his half of the sandwich and the refreshing glass of tea.

"Mm, mm, this is good. It was either this or my wife's forbidden chicken salad."

Donnie wiped a smear of mustard from his chin.

"Un hum, un hum." Was all Damien could mutter between bites.

Before you knew it, the whole sandwich and iced tea had been consumed. One loud belch sealed their state of contentment.

"That wasn't bad at all, in fact, it was downright delicious." Damien said.

"That my friend was my famous Double-D, Donnie Detonator. Of course, it would've been much better had it not been hours old."

"It was definitely alright by me. It well served its purpose."

"Uh oh, we forgot to say grace. Now, I know I'm glad my wife's not here."

"Now don't go getting all religious on me. What's the world coming to? Every time you turn around, people quoting Scripture . . . Jesus this, and Jesus that. To tell you the truth, my boy, I'm sick of it."

"Whoa Nelly!" Donnie said. "If I'd known a full stomach would make you so anti-religious, I would've let your old butt starve."

"I don't call taking a stance on overkill blaspheming." Damien said.

"Well, usually a person is running from something when they're that anti-spiritual."

"Me, running? From what dare I ask?"

"Something say, like maybe a calling perhaps?"

"Hell yeah, I've been called alright, everything but a child of God by my wife! I heard a voice, but it surely wasn't God's."

Damien shucked his teeth and turned away.

Donnie placed a ball on the floor and grabbed a nine iron from his golf bag. He lightly tapped and sent the ball scurrying across the room.

"I'm she sure had grounds to."

"She did at that." Damien stated. "But you brought it up, remember? And God did make all mankind."

"So I did . . . what was I thinking?" Donnie said without looking up.

"When did men become such wimps? Now just look at who caused my man to lose all he had." Damien went on. "A woman, a brotha was sitting phat! I'm telling you, we men were meant to rule the world."

Donnie looked up questionably, wanting to know exactly where this was leading. He never expected this worldly man to dive so deeply into religion.

"Bring it down a notch will you? What's gotten into you anyway?"

"Sorry, I got a little carried away."

"Dude you got more patches than my grandmother's quilt. You hadn't wanted to talk religion, now look at you. I can't shut you up."

"Well, that's something else you don't know about me, I am a well learned man." Damien said proudly.

You trying to say you know enough to exegete the Word or to eisegete it?"

A puzzled look came over Damian's face, prompting Donnie to further explain.

"Was it what you read into it, or, was it what you drew from it? Duhh! You understand now?"

"Okay, I didn't tell you before but, I am a preacher's kid, so I do know something about the Word."

"Get out of here!" Donnie exclaimed. "Do your parents know about their boy-ii?"

"Both my parents are deceased."

"Sorry man, that was uncalled for. I was just ribbing you a bit."

Then to get back on a lighter note he brought up the morning's occurrences once again.

"Besides I told you weird thing's been happening around here. First Etta Mae's weird dream and then close encounters of the third kind, so I'd best stop talking.

I can't say who might just pop up." He glanced eerily around the room, and then playfully added. "Like you."

"You jive turkey, you're stuffed with something, but it sure ain't cornbread!"

"You thought I was kidding." Donnie said laughing. I watched it play out from my hiding place in the closet."

He was too embarrassed to say that he had actually peed his pants in the hallway.

"You talking about somebody scared." Donnie grabbed at his chest. "Why I thought I's going to meet my Maker."

Damien doesn't know what to make of this man and his ever changing antics. From what little time he had spent here he just couldn't figure if Donnie was ever serious or if he humored him. But on this matter, to be safe he chose to disbelieve. He nervously paced the floor, challenging Donnie's words.

"I thought you were kidding, when you talked that shit earlier." Damien shakily said. "Lord what have I walked into?"

"So be careful, Eve's been up in here today."

Donnie continued to weave his tale. He was amused at the discomfort of his houseguest.

If truth be told, ghost stories have always terrified Damien. He recalled how his grandmother and her girlfriends would sit and talk for hours about how hants would be in ceilings of old haunted houses. How way-farers would stop nightly to rest only to be confronted by the disembodied spirits.

It would seem to Damien, having been blessed with a vivid

imagination, he himself would end up being the unfortunate traveler. He would become so engrossed in the tale-weaving that fear would grip him with an iron fist.

It hadn't help that he would have to climb dark stairs alone to sleep in a dark bedroom. That's when the many dead bodies he had witnessed lain out in the sanctuary of his father's church would come to his mind.

"Shut up, will you!" Damien felt a cold chill run up and down his back."

"Oka-ay then . . . moving on . . . ." Donnie said. He realized he had somehow actually spooked the now trembling man that stood before him. "But don't say I didn't warn you."

"Look here, I know what you're trying to do, but I'm not buying it." Damien said.

"You're not buying what?"

"That same bull you were talking earlier when I knocked on your door. Thinking I was the devil or some stupid crap."

"Oh well, suit yourself Mr. I Don't-Believe-He's-Risen." Donnie said.

"If Adam hadn't had that surgery you know we would still be in that garden." Damien said.

"You know doubting Thomas does not have a thing on you, dude."

"Come to think of it, did Adam even ask God for that woman?" Damien said. All the supernatural talk was getting the best of the man.

"You back on that again? Didn't I say to be careful what you talk about?"

Donnie pinches the tip of his nose when he is annoyed or in a position of uncertainty.

"And that's something you'll have to ask Etta Mae, she can tell you better than I can."

"Come, oh great A-dam."

Damian didn't fully believe anything out of the ordinary would occur, so he pressed the issue further. "Come, oh great one. Ooo-ooo!"

"Fool! Would you shut up?"

Donnie's nose really got a work out as he tried unsuccessfully to shush the unbeliever.

"You think you're funny, don't you? But if you keep playing around, my man Adam just might answer your call."

Chapter Fifteen

Delilah's afternoon walk proved to be more challenging than she had anticipated. The hot blazing afternoon sun beat down it seemed to her relentlessly.

The three quarters length jacket she'd worn was moist with sweat. The silk purple blouse worn beneath the gray rayon caprice ensemble clung to her wet back wet.

She slid the jacket off her shoulders and tied it around her waist. She wiped the beads of sweat from her forehead as her pace slowed. Why had she worn these between the toe 2" sandals?

Note to self: "Think foot comfort before fashion before deciding to tour a neighborhood.

The $169.00 Ted Nardy sneakers that lay haphazardly discarded on the bedroom floor would've been a better choice, even though they wouldn't have complimented her outfit.

"But no! I just had to be cute!" She chided herself.

The thought of turning around to retrieve the comfortable footwear had crossed her mind, but she decided instead to press on. It would only be a short walk anyway.

A power walker that had stepped onto the sidewalk after doing her stretches approached her with wide determined strides.

She had smiled, but it was actually more of a smirk when her eyes casually took in Dee's inappropriate footwear.

"Hello."

The walker muttered as she side stepped the fashionable stroller to begin her jaunt. Dee returned a forced greeting.

"Hi."

She stole a glance over her shoulder in time to see the woman in full stride, tearing up the sidewalk.

Dismayed, she kicked the backless shoes off her feet hoping to ease the ache in her arch. But the rough, hot surface beneath her feet wasn't anything she had bargained for.

"Ouch! I swear!" Dee slipped her foot into the slides once again. "I guess it's better to ache than to burn."

As she rounded a corner, blaring pulsating music accompanied by voices of rowdy revelers spilled out into the street.

All makes and models of vehicles crammed the driveway of the tri-level home. The barely accessible street was lined with cars parked haphazardly. She could see and smell the smoke rising from a bar-b-cue grill on the back patio.

"Party over here, ain't bleep over there!" A raucous reveler could be heard declaring from inside. "Hoot, hoot!"

"Humph, it sounds like the party has just gotten started in there."

Dee's quick reaction saved her from a rear collision with four rambunctious teenagers. Their skateboard's grinding wheels and exhilarating laughter only added to the noisy afternoon ruckus.

Dee's foot discomfort soon gave way to intrigue, as she watched a beaming young father holding hands with his wife carry an infant seat to an idling vehicle.

The young man gingerly reached inside and smoothed the pink blanket. Once the carrier was securely locked in the rear seat, he went around and opened the car door for his wife, planting a kiss on her lips as he did so.

The smiling young wife waved eagerly before she settled into the cooled air conditioned interior. Dee returned the greeting with a hesitant wave but quickly averted her gaze.

After she had awakened from her nap, Dee prepared herself to get out into the fresh air. She'd left the house an hour or so after her sister and friend. She hadn't cared to accompany them on their Saturday's outing.

Who would want to be a third wheel? It's probably something they do religiously anyway.

The jaw dropping scene she had witnessed in her New York apartment was continually on rewind in her mind.

How could he do that to me . . . better yet, how could he be . . . ?"

She couldn't bring herself to form the word. It almost, always stuck in her throat. "In the arms of . . . not another woman, but a . . . man."

"There, I said it."

You think you know a person. I thought I knew everything about Damien. I know his likes and dislikes. How he prefers dry toast as opposed to butter drenched."

She and her husband had, she thought a pleasurable relationship. Damien always knew where and just how to touch her. That's what was so puzzling about the whole thing.

She had been slowly walking for some time before realizing her cheeks were wet with tears.

Why the tears, are they from anger, or are they from the hurt and the humiliation I'm feeling?

Thank goodness, in all my marriages, I never had to embody

the sheer pain that's cutting me so deeply now. I was always the one who chose to end each commitment."

The casual stroller distractedly plucked away at a wild dandelion blossom she'd stooped to pick.

I guess I'll never know why it's so hard for me to form lasting relationships.

"Til death do us part," was the vow I took each and every time. Yet, I always walked away.

Of course, I can give myself credit for the two that left me bereft. But even then I could only mourn for a short time.

An unusual phenomenon occurred as she descended a sloping hill, still deep in thought. A cloud like haze enshrouded her. The morning haze should have long since burned off in the smoldering heat.

Not only had she become disoriented, but a blast from a honking horn, caused her to lose her footing. Dee shakily watched as the phantom car sped on its way, oblivious to her pounding heart.

The haze began to lift, and before her stood a towering white edifice. A marquee in the shape of a well, made of the finest white marble was erected on the manicured lawn. The front of the well was emblazoned with black onyx letters that read **Re-Dig the Wells of Jubilation Worship Center.**

"Now that's saying a mouth full. I belong to RWJWC."

She laughed at the thought of having to relay that to a person.

Services began at 8:00 Sunday mornings, according to the marquee, then again at 11:00. Wednesday's were reserved for Bible Study/Prayer Meeting, at 7:00 p.m.

The massive white structure sat on ten acres of manicured green lawn, dotted here and there with lush myrtle and ash trees.

The four squared building was identical on its four sides. Each entrance was flanked by three magnificent ten feet high white double doors.

Twelve doors total allowed access into the building, three on the East, three on the North, three on the South, and still, three on the West.

Four straight unadorned white columns were arrayed across the aperture of each white stoned porch. To a disoriented being, they would appear to be giant guardian angels defying anyone or anything to defile the space between them.

The majestic columns supported a massive roof measuring 106,500 square feet, housing a grand steeple that soared dizzyingly; it appeared to the awe struck observer, to the highest heavens.

For the sake of going green, cylindrical solar panels lined each side of the flat roof, giving the much needed energy saving support. Well placed skylights saturated the sanctuary below with natural light from above.

I wonder if this is where my sister and brother-in-law worship. I know Etta Mae, but not so much Donnie is always in somebody's church.

She stood there for quite some time, lost in thought. From her standpoint, the wide white paneled doors appeared to beckon her wayward soul to enter deep into its holistic walls.

"My, my, my, how majestic and pure you are in all your splendor!" She voiced aloud.

"It could very well be the most important decision you'll ever make in your lifetime."

The gawking New Yorker swung sharply around, startled beyond belief by a deep baritone voice.

A tall, broadly built black Adonis, the color of smooth, dark chocolate impeccably dressed, she guessed to be in his early fifties had exited a glistening white automobile.

The white tailored suit made of the finest silk appeared to all but shimmer in the bright sun light. Her eyes followed the long, lean legs down to the whitest of white Italian leather shoes.

Short hair brushed into a perfected 360 wave pattern, graying at the temples, framed a square-jawed face.

A well-trimmed salt and pepper mustache sat between a broad nose and full dark lips. Those same ample lips parted in the most welcoming smile, revealing perfect white teeth.

Oh my, his parents must have paid a fortune for those pearly whites.

Dee thought it to be virtually impossible for the perfect choppers to belong to any human.

She suddenly found her small trembling hand become engulfed in a warm vacuum. But just as quickly, she withdrew it and absently wiped her hand on the front of her tailored shorts.

This gentleman's presence is unnerving. Donnie had warned her to be careful. She stole another quick look at his face. There's something about his eyes.

"Hello, young lady, I'm Master Prophet, Eli Cummings." He watched the nervous woman closely. "You're new around here, aren't you? I mean, I've never seen you in this neighborhood before."

"Ah, uh, yes, I mean no . . . I mean n-no I'm not." Dee stammered.

"Yes, or no . . . which is it?"

"No, I'm not from here. I just flew in town on yesterday in fact, from New York. I'm visiting my sister and her husband."

She looked past the tall figure to the street and wondered how she could escape this creepy close encounter.

"Et-Etta Mae and Donnie LeRoy Smith. Etta Mae's my oldest sister."

"I know them. Your sister is a staunch warrior on the battlefield for the Lord. Now, as for Donnie, well . . ."

"Oh, so you're their pastor, I mean they are members here?"

"No, they are not members of this church, but what is good about it all, is that they do belong to God's Church."

"Oh, I just thought . . ."

"And what about you?" He sternly asked. "What church are you affiliated with?"

Oh no, here we go. Now he's gone and done it. Why'd he have to go and ask that question?

The prophet patiently waited for the answer to his suspicions.

"W-ell . . . ." She slowly responded. "How can I put this? When I was little, my grandmother took us to . . . in fact I, ah, that is, w-we were baptized there. I-I mean, my sisters and I were baptized at St. Stephen's Missionary Baptist Church, in Carterville, North Carolina."

"Oh, I see . . . now that wasn't so hard, now was it?" the prophet asked.

"Your grandmother obviously did her part and that was to teach you about the Lord, but the rest; accepting Him into your heart was up to you."

He said this, fully knowing the woman's belief system was on shaky grounds from the start. He had only asked her the soul-searching question in order for her to put a voice on her stance on faith or lack thereof.

Her agnostic view of God meant that somewhere deep down she had once believed, but had rationalized at some time or other, in her life that He didn't exist.

"Huh?" Dee fidgeted and looked down. The uneasiness she felt had become more pronounced each passing moment.

"I-I guess y-you could say that."

"Now your sister Cynthia . . ."

"H-how do you know about Cyndi? I didn't tell you I had a sister by that name!"

She began to back away, ready to bolt from the strange man's all-knowing presence.

"Why would a good and merciful God allow your parents to perish?" That's the question you two wanted answered."

"Well, if He's so good then why would He?"

"Delilah," the prophet began, "from the years you were with Mrs. Collins, your grandmother, I know you learned the adversary, the devil was the only one who "comes to steal, to kill, and to destroy."

No one ever stops to blame the one responsible for the catastrophes in the world, but instead, prefers to blame God.

If it is written that, "Jesus came so that we may have life, and have it more abundantly. Then could you please tell me how death and destruction could come from those words."

The prophet watched her mull the words over in her head. He led the trembling woman to a nearby bench embossed with an advertisement.

"Only Heaven's water is purer. Come! Drink from the Well; you'll never thirst again!" They sat down.

"There's a word of knowledge for you, Mrs. Delilah Carol Collins Melvin Cox Williams Simmons Jefferson Whitman, the prophet said without pausing to breathe.

"And it is . . . you're only bound by what you allow to bind you."

She rose to flee, but the astonished woman found it virtually impossible to pull away. She was more restrained by his knowledge of her life's history than by an actual physical grip.

"You sound exactly like my sister! Is there no end to my torment?"

"Yes," he said, "there is an end, but only you know how, and only you know when. The power is yours."

"The power is mine?" She asked through tears. "You mean I have the power to lose this heavy burden I've been carrying of my husband's betrayal?" You're saying I have the power of freeing myself of non-commitment? I have the power to—

"To forgive your husband of his infidelity, for the hurt, the shame, and the humiliation he's caused you? Yes! Delilah, the power lies within you. And He is called the Holy Spirit."

"What do you mean, the Holy Spirit?" she questioned defiantly, "I don't even believe there is a God let alone a spirit that's holy and supposedly living in me. And besides, you don't even know what that man did to me!"

"You're wrong, I do know, and I also know where he is now."

"Now? Right now . . . you're telling me you know where my trifling husband is right this very moment?"

"Yes, my dear, I do."

"Oh; okay, so you got it like that. I'm impressed, but forgive me if I don't ask where he is, because I don't care."

"Yes, you do care, but at the moment you're thinking with your emotions."

"Yes, I am angry and I'll never forgive that traitor."

"Even you must know that there's no sin too great or too small that is not covered under the blood of the Savior, Jesus Christ."

"W-well, forgiving someone is a pretty tall order in my book."

"No, you're wrong, but there is one sin that is un-forgivable and you, unfortunately, are treading dangerous waters."

"Oh, and just how exactly am I doing that, may I ask?" She stood up and so did he.

"Simply by your choice to hold on to the unsavory belief that God doesn't exist, or your wanting proof that He does. You were taught to know better."

"So tell me, where's all this love He's supposed to have for us?"

Ironically, the stranger already knew that the brave front the troubled woman displayed was nothing more than a safety net she'd erected to keep from falling.

"You have felt Him tugging at your heart-string, but you continue to be in a state of denial and saying no to his Holy Spirit. And *that*, my dear child, is called blasphemy, the unpardonable sin."

"So, what exactly makes it unpardonable?"

"Think about it would you! When a person confesses his sins and asks Christ into his heart, that person is then saved. The Spirit of Christ comes to dwell within his spirit.

Fortunately, he no longer listens to his soul-man but instead listens to his spirit-man. That's how we'll able to choose between right and wrong."

He stared intensely into her eyes, as he continued to explain.

"The Holy Spirit is our conscience. However, if you never ask Him in, or believe on Him, then when you die, and since your sins haven't been pardoned; guess where you end up?"

"Hell?"

"In Hell."

"Oh . . . since you know me so well," Dee contended. "I don't have to tell you that I also don't believe in Hell either.

Like I said before; since your God loves us so much then why would He send His loved ones to torment?"

"Young lady, do you hear yourself? Do you hear what you are saying?"

"Yes! I know exactly what I'm saying, and I'm not the only one who's said it either. So there!"

"Well," what you just said proves to me that you do know deep down in your soul that the God you supposedly have rejected is a good God.

You know in your heart that He does not send anyone to torment, because He said in 3 John 2 "Beloved, concerning all things, I wish that you may prosper and be in good health, even as your soul prospers."

"Who *or* what exactly are you?" Dee asked, unable to refute the remark. "Are you an angel?"

"Who, or what do you think I am?"

"I don't have a clue, that's why I asked you." She took a step backwards. Something she seemed to be doing a lot while she conversed with this stranger.

"Well, in that case, I can be who or whatever you want me to be at this particular moment." He offered. "I do know that right now you need me to be a listening and non-judgmental ear that can shed light in your darkness. To give answers to the burning questions that's tearing you up inside."

She sensed a quieting in her spirit and pondered the many questions lying dormant. The stranger remained quiet, patiently waiting for the onslaught to burst forth.

"Okay then, since you seem to have all the ready answers . . . . pray tell me how this mind, body and spirit thing works. Are not they all the same?"

"May I take a seat, please?" The prophet sat down once again, not waiting for a response.

"Oh, is it going to be that long and drawn out?"

He simply looked at the inquisitive woman and patted the seat next to him. She hesitantly sat down, but left considerable space between them.

"You see, my dear, man is made up of three components." He began. "Spirit, soul and body—

"Duhh!" Dee interjected. "You don't have to be an Einstein to know that."

"Allow me to finish, please." The stranger said. "And if I'm not mistaken, I believe I've already covered that."

"Oops . . . sorry, I wasn't listening then."

"Apology accepted. Now then, when you're a believer, God then dwells in you and communicates with your regenerated spirit, which then saturates your soul, allowing man to become transformed to express Him. Romans 12: 2b "Be ye transformed by the renewing of your mind."

"Wow! So, let me see if I got this straight." Dee finally said. "If I understand you correctly, you're actually saying . . . .

When or if my body is occupied and directed by the Spirit of God, then His Spirit talks to me through my spirit, and uses my body for His purpose."

"That's right. You get life with a purpose."

"Wow! That's some deep shi—

"Uh mm! Now, the reason I said you are in danger of blaspheming, is because you've personally chosen to disconnect your phone line so to speak.

"My phone line, you say?"

"Yes, your phone line, and that, however, could very well be your answer to finding inner peace."

"Like understanding why I find myself marrying and marrying again?" She naively stated.

The prophet remained quiet, but he instead opted to allow the perplexed woman to draw her own conclusions. It seemed like an eternity before she spoke again.

"Speaking of marriage, how can God help me with the situation I'm finding myself in now?"

She posed the question to herself more so than to the stranger. Again, her pondering question was met with total silence.

"Oh, I see, now you're giving me the old silent treatment."

"Some of life's many questions are only meant to be answered by the one who's asking them." He finally said.

"Albeit, I can tell you this . . . do you remember the slogan made popular some few years ago?"

"To what slogan are you referring?"

"WWJD. What would Jesus do? Remember?"

"Hummm . . . what would Jesus do indeed? Hmmm." She carefully pondered before answering.

The stranger patiently waited for her answer.

"Let's see . . . I think . . . He would forgive; yes that's exactly what He'd do. He would simply forgive. Now isn't that just like Him?"

"And there you have it."

The prophet proclaimed, smiling warmly. The words which he had finally heard from a woman who'd lost her way were music to his ears.

The now enlightened woman was on the verge of re-digging the well of her salvation. The well her beloved grandmother had once helped her to dig. But his jubilation was short lived.

"Hel-lo! In case you haven't noticed, I'm not Him, I'm not Jesus!" Dee's statement had dispelled his assumptions. "That's way too tall of an order!"

"Not if you would just allow His Spirit to communicate with your spirit, it isn't."

Her statement had bought the prophet back to the task at hand. He went on to further explain.

"It can only be done by asking for the Lord for the Spirit of Forgiveness."

"Oh damn . . . I mean, darn!"

Unbridled tears ran down the woman's face and fell on the expensive silk blouse.

"Now look what I've done! This is virgin silk!" She attempted to explain. "Water and real silk doesn't mix you know."

"Yes, I know, but you my dear have much to think about and much soul searching to do."

"I do?"

"Yes, you do . . . And I'm afraid I'll have to leave you to do just that."

He started to rise from the bench. "I pray you peace and I pray you understanding."

"Wait! Don't go!"

She instinctively reached out to block his rising. A frantic moment was frozen in time. Finally, the prophet resettled onto the bench.

Thoughts of despair ran through his mind. He had hoped that just maybe, a break-through by the hurting soul seated beside him would have occurred.

"It's . . . it's just that I don't know what to do about my husband."

"What about him; him and mankind in general for that matter?"

'I'm . . . I'm just lost as to what decision to make is all."

Her head was bowed so low, the next question came out in a whisper.

"What made him do this to me?" Sobbing, she lifted her bowed head and cried out. "Jesus! Help Me!"

The Man of God offered her his white handkerchief. He shifted uneasily in his seat before attempting to give any semblance of an explanation. However, it pleased him dearly to hear the unbeliever call on a name she probably had not called on since childhood. Yes, there was always hope.

"Romans One." He began. "Around verse twenty-five or so; Man, God's creation, through the Fall had become vain and took on the attributes of Satan.

Though man knew God, he did not thank Him or glorify Him. And in doing so, the Creator gave man up to the lusts of his heart so that he could dishonor his own body."

"W-*what?*" The increased wrinkles and frown on the woman's forehead alerted the prophet that he needed to break the wording down to her level of understanding.

"I said all that to say this; man fell in love with himself, therefore, he chose to love what looked like himself over the One who had created him."

"You mean . . ."

"Wait!" He said. "I mean that man was given over to uncleanness, passions of dishonor and a disapproved mind, because through the fault of the enemy; man didn't really see God for who He is.

The Creator is not the author of confusion, but you can't say that about the enemy. The enemy's mind will have a man thinking he's a woman, and a woman thinking that she's a man. In their mind's eye, they may think they can only love what looks like them. Scripture tells us, "Let the mind be in you that was also in Christ Jesus."

So, if you don't have His mind, then it's easier for the mind of the enemy to be supplanted in one's thoughts."

"Whew . . . it's all too complicated for me." Dee stated.

"Well maybe this will help you. To think in the flesh or to be carnal minded, a man can lie with a man, and a woman can lie with a woman with no qualms."

Dee finally understood, but thought it to be a bit too farfetched.

"Look around you, is not man the only creation who can choose to go against what he was designed for?"

"Hey, now that you've put it that way . . . man is the only hardheaded creation there is!" Satan realizes that and only comes after man and not animals, per se, to do the opposite of what God designed him to do or be."

She slapped her hands together with excitement and shouted.

"Hot damn! Oo, sorry."

"Simply because Man was made in the image of God, and if Satan's the enemy of God, then guess what he is to us."

"That old piece of slime!" Dee shouted.

"Now, I must say, in all fairness . . . to be truthfully honest, sin is sin and no one sin is greater than another. Fornication, adultery, murder, incest and slander are no less sin in the eyes of God than homosexuality. Although he did call that certain act, an abomination.

"But to let man tell it, homosexuality is not sinful." Dee snickered.

"The devil is a lie, and the father of lies." Prophet Cummings shook his head in disbelief.

"And people wonder why the Word says "My people perish from the lack of knowledge." And oh, by the way, that scripture spoke of the lack of spiritual knowledge."

"Maybe that's how judges are passing laws to legalize everything under the sun." Dee added.

"Hmmm . . . well, since you said that, then I can only quote 2 Chronicles 19: 6 "Consider carefully what you do, because you are not judging for man but for the Lord, who is with you whenever you give a verdict." In other words, "judge carefully" is the warning to the moral decision makers.

The two had been talking for well over two hours. Fatigue weighed heavily on them both. They both thought heavily on the argumentative topics that had been discussed.

Just by knowing what was needed to make things right between herself and God caused Dee's head to sink even lower. She just could not bring herself to utter the fateful words of "Father, forgive me, for I have sinned."

Prophet Cummings watched the expressions of indecision play across the woman's countenance. He knew she was on the verge of denouncing the benighted views she had once held, and were now ready to drink from the Well. He would not be surprised at the remark he would hear come from the now enlightened disciple.

A sense of calmness settled over her anxious spirit. There was just something about this man of God. But . . . she couldn't exactly put her finger on it.

"You know . . . I feel like the "woman at the well." She finally said to the stranger. "You have surely given me living water to drink. Now out of my belly shall surely flow oceans, not rivers, but oceans of this living water! I must go now!" She rose to leave.

"I must *run,* and I must *tell* everyone how sweet the water is in this Well from which I just drank."

And she did just that, leaving her long ago discarded shoes behind, as she did so. For some reason, she had been unable to keep them on her feet. The luscious green grass had felt like velvet under her feet, soothing and comforting. After she had run a few feet away, the now liberated woman looked down and realized she was shoeless.

Another cloudy haze had mysteriously descended when she

turned back. It was so thick Dee could barely make out the tall figure that stood in the space she'd just vacated.

She also remembered that she hadn't thanked the Master Prophet for the Water he had verbally poured into her life. She ran back through the mist.

The Stranger welcomed her with open arms and the two embraced. She felt so protected in his arms and thought how she could've stayed there forever.

Finally, the embrace was broken, and they both stepped away. No words were spoken as she looked deep into his eyes for the very first time.

The woman's eyes widened as she seemingly drowned in the pools of love she found there. To her his eyes were deeper than the deepest sea.

"My Child." He simply said and took a hold of Dee's hand. She fell to her knees.

Extreme emotions over shadowed the kneeling woman. The repenting woman sobbed uncontrollably while she held tightly to his comforting hands. She let go of one hand long enough to wipe the tears from her eyes.

She no longer saw the brilliant white leather shoes as she looked down, but instead, she saw bare, nail scarred-feet. Dee raised her head and quickly inspected his wrists.

To her astonishment, there were nail prints. Suddenly everything came into focus, leaving the former agnostic to cry out.

"My Lord and My God! Forgive me and come into my life!"

Those same nail scarred hands lifted the forlorn woman to her feet.

"Delilah Collins, you were forgiven a long time ago." He said. "My peace I give you and my peace I leave you."

"I-I was, even after I denied you?"

"There was once a friend of mine who denied me three times . . . and I forgave him three times."

"So, what you're saying is . . . you never tire of forgiving us."

"Yes, that is true."

"No . . . that is love." The delivered woman corrected.

He smiled the warmest smile ever, before he said to her.

"Go now, daughter and do what is right in your heart."

Dee covered her face with her hands as uncontrollable sobs racked her delivered soul. But this time these were soothing tears of joy. When next she looked up, it was apparent she was alone. Even the magnificent, white edifice had disappeared.

Ironically, it didn't matter to her. She did not feel alone, because somewhere in the recesses of her spirit she heard the words; "I'll never leave you, nor forsake you." The woman now knew the Stranger was no longer a stranger. He was her God!

Suddenly the world seemed brighter; her soul felt lighter. Birds chirped, and vibrant colored butterflies flickered about. With her head thrown back in total abandonment, Dee found herself spinning around and around.

The blue sky was filled with enormous white cumulus clouds. She stopped abruptly. It suddenly registered that she still hadn't thanked the Man of God. So, she uttered those very words, and cried out with a loud voice.

"Thank you! Thank you Jesus!"

From out of nowhere she heard an audible voice.

"Daughter; thank you for allowing me to bless you. Welcome back to the fold."

I may never know just how long I would have gone before stopping to realize that my Redeemer lives.

She became so over whelmed with the sense of gratitude that an unrehearsed shout of *"Hallelujah,"* exploded from her lips.

"*Thank you! Thank you! Thank you!*

Dee shouted from the top of her voice. Then she picked up her shoes and danced down the street with the tune, *I Can See Clearly Now,* the rain is gone actively playing in her head.

Chapter Sixteen

"Are you finally ready to tell me about what's really going on with you?" Etta Mae asked Tonika. "You and Stephanie had a secret code going on back there for a minute. And don't think I didn't notice."

"Why, what-ev-a' do you mean, Miss Et-ta?" Tonika said in her best southern drawl. "I don't have a clue what you're talking 'bout."

Tonika felt as if there were a lot she didn't know. This is so unusual, I share everything with my friend she thought to herself, but this time it's different. For one thing I haven't even come to grips with the bombshell myself.

"When you're ready, my friend, you will tell me, but only when you're ready." Etta Mae gave the trembling hand a gentle squeeze. "And I'll be here when you are."

Etta Mae could sense the turmoil her friend was going through. From what little was shared this morning, she knew it definitely had something to do with Josh.

"You truly are a dear friend. Thanks for understanding."

Etta Mae gave Tonika's shoulder a reassuring rub.

"Hmmm, that's funny, look at that, I never noticed that store before."

Tonika' eyes followed her friend's gaze to a shop seductively staged with women's intimate apparel. The name on the front of the store was *Surreptitious.*

Tonika moved over to the window for a closer inspection. A barely there pink see-through garment seductively arrayed on a mulatto toned mannequin dominated the window display.

Shades of red dominated the interior of the boutique. Red delicate lace bras in the form of strapless, mini-misers, convertibles and wonder-wires, were amply displayed throughout the show room. "*A sure natural fit for any body size,*" was how the caption read for the delicate apparels.

Revealing panties, bustiers in animal prints and solids lay folded on rounded red organza covered tables. Etta Mae took a seat on a nearby bench, and picked up a discarded brochure.

She began to casually thumb through it. The featured cover was emblazoned with intimate articles of clothing.

"Only she knows where her power is hidden." The sassy slogan read.

"*Lingerie meant to be worn under any formative business suit, or elegant gown, giving the wearer the feeling of power to take charge, and most importantly, feel seductive.*"

Surreptitious, meaning hidden things were boldly printed on the vibrant red and black pamphlet cover. It was a brochure from the intimate apparel boutique before them. It featured the same articles of clothing displayed in the window.

The boutique it seemed was founded by a Jessie Devlin, of Lower Crescent, New York, in collaboration with his wife, Wicca. The Devlin's design of intimate apparel was highly prized among their risqué clientele.

Fantasy designs made up a large portion of the Devlin's line, accommodating the most daring at heart.

French maidens, red-hot she devils, leopard skins, bunnies, you name it. Alluring bras and panties crafted only for the bold and the beautiful were the mainstay of the collection.

The *Jazzy Jezzie* Line, a cohesive collection of red seductive, alluring, matte nylon and Chantilly lace bras, thongs, boy-shorts and beyond were the most popular items sold. Each piece was delicately constructed to mix or match. This line of intimate wear embodied the very essence of its namesake, *Jezebel*.

Etta Mae was flabbergasted by a warning written in small print. **Caution: A sudden feeling of domination may overtake the unbridled wearer of this garment. Be careful to never expose the undergarments to sunlight when worn.**

"Ooo-wee! Those *Jazzie Jezzies* are some dangerous undies!" Etta Mae shared the pamphlet with Tonika.

"Look at this . . . they almost come to life it looks like, if the light catches them while you're wearing them."

"My, my, that's stupid!"

Tonika took the pamphlet. Her mouth dropped open in disbelief.

"I tell you what girlfriend; anytime any drawers of mine come to life by themselves, you better shoot me dead!" The look of shock on her friend's face led her to add. "For real though, I ain't lying."

"Okay, I can do that for you, but just remember, you asked."

Laughter was shared, and then Etta Mae paused for a moment.

"Those 'Jazzie Jezzies' are something fierce, not unlike their namesake, I might add."

She chuckled to herself before commenting on the antics of the biblical character.

As the two ladies are talking, a miraculous transformation was taking place near the store's front entrance. A store mannequin had begun to transpose.

"Tonika, now you do know that Eve wasn't the only woman in the Bible who had her man under thumb, don't you?"

"You mean there's more?"

"Yes mam, you bet there was more. There was that woman named Jezebel!"

"Jezebel, I've heard about her, just last week . . ."

"Umph! Now that girl was b-b-bad to the bone!" Etta Mae continued.

"Do you think it's safe to bring up . . . you know, her name?" Tonika did a quick glance around. "I mean, you know what happened earlier."

"Now, my girl Jezzie was queen of all the vixens. She got things done without her man even knowing how it was done. Lies, were how she did it, you know. My girl was a straight faced liar!"

"What makes you say that?" "Because, honey . . . Jezebel was so evil, even Jesus talked about her in Revelation 2."

"Well, she must've been bad then, if Jesus talked about her. She probably ranked right up there with those Pharisees and the Sadducees."

"Look at you! Go on with you bad self!" Etta Mae exclaimed.

"You see, I do have retaining power."

"Yes, I see . . . but back to the scarlet lady; now it's said if you're not careful her spirit will take over your body even today. And it doesn't matter if you're a man or a woman."

"Oh, so that explains why it says if you wear her namesake, you're bound to become a dominatrix of sorts." Tonika reasoned. "Ummm, maybe, that's the answer to my problem. Note to self; buy 'Jezzie' wear!"

"Oh, I wouldn't do that if I were you." Etta Mae warned. "Why would you want to look like a floozy anyway? You know Black women are already stereotyped as Jezebels!"

"Are you serious? Etta, I swear you're a walking, talking encyclopedia." Tonika said. "I didn't know that. And where'd you get it from anyhow?"

"You may don't know it, but I do read other books besides the Bible."

"I know you're well read, so lay it on me, sistah. What's my lesson today?"

"Well, for your moment in Black History, I'm quoting something I gleaned from a paper written by a Dr. David Pilgrim at the Ferris State University's Jim Crow Museum.

He called it the Jezebel Stereotype. According to the paper, Jezebel was depicted as a "Black woman with an insatiable appetite. Stereotyping black women as Jezebels were used during slavery as a rationalization for sexual relations between slavers, and their slaves."

Apparently, that's the reason we were raped by massa whenever and wherever. You get me?"

"Whew! How can that be?" Tonika inquired. "You mean to say Jezebel was powerful and horny, too? Now that's a destructive combination!"

Tonika thought of the conversation she'd had with Edna Brown two weeks ago.

Edna had given her a printout on the wiles of the horrible woman. She hadn't taken the time to read it but had stuffed it in her purse, hoping to look it over later.

"Tonika, you are too much!"

"Okay, here is what else it said. "Black women were thought of in Jim Crow's days as being lascivious by nature."

"The adjectives that were used to categorize us were: seductive, alluring, worldly, beguiling, tempting and lewd.

Now get this, white women were thought of as self-respectful, self-controlled, and modest."

"It would say that about them. But I thought you were only called that if you were light skinned, you know, mullatto, with long hair, and a coke bottle shape. And oh, don't forget voluptuous red lips."

Tonika's pouted lips made both women chuckle. They are so engrossed in their conversation, that neither noticed the eerie figure that moved towards them.

"True 'dat, true 'dat," Etta Mae laughingly commented, "but to massa, any female form, no matter what she looked like, was just a dark crevice to sink his flag pole in."

"Ummph, and my poor foremothers were called every name in the book. Now, I learned they were even called Jezebels." Tonika commented.

"Shucks girl, who knows, maybe massa put bags over their heads."

"Let's just say, over our less attractive foremother's heads. Oh, and to be fair, that paper also stated that your foremothers were even raped by your own forefathers. And since it was the norm, our poor mothers didn't have a defense."

"Umph, umph, umph," Tonika grunted, and solemnly shook her head. "My people, my people!"

Dark blank eyes with eyelids painted every hue of the rainbow stared pointedly at the two unsuspecting women.

A chained gold nose ring that reached from the left ear to a nostril adorned a smooth flawless face. The headdress and jewelry told of her regal position. The small frame, average figure of a woman was covered from head to toe, in red chiffon as the tradition of a Phoenician princess warranted.

Thin pale arms that once hung lifeless ended in long tapered manicured fingers painted the most brilliant red.

The ladies were startled when the airways became filled with the pulsating beat of *Bad Girls*. The loud music had over taken the soothing piano concerto that had been continuously playing.

Gold ornaments worn on the formidable phantom figure's ankles jingled distractedly as she stealthily made her way toward the befuddled women.

"Uh oh, let the games begin!" Tonika watched terrified and yelled over the pounding beat. "I bet cha' anything that's old Jezzie!"

"Well, if it isn't the Painted Lady herself . . . in the flesh!" Etta Mae yelled back, with both fingers in her ears.

The music died down as Jezebel began to speak. She paced to and fro in front of the women.

"I know, I know, you two ladies probably think of me as the hussy of all hussies. Now, don't you?" She blazed at the startled women. *"But honey, if you had a man like mine, you would do the same as I did."*

"Well, if you want to go there, you won't get any argument from us."

Tonika returned the stare and thought of something the angels always said in the Bible when they visited a human.

"I have a question for you. How come you spirits don't ever say, "Fear not," like the angels? No, you just show up and begin to speak as if someone's been expecting you."

"Mrs. Gibbons, I presume?" Jezebel asked. *"My name alone as you know, strikes fear in people's hearts as it is so why would I waste words on something so trivial?"* Smiling wickedly, she shouted. *"Boo!"* Then she went on to ask. *"So, are you scared or not?"*

Tonika's hands flew to her mouth, stifling a gasp.

"Is my name popular with you spirits today or something?"

"*Yes, I have to say it has been discussed a time or two.*" Jezebel retorted flippantly.

"By whom?"

"*It doesn't matter; I just came to enlighten you. You two were talking about me just then and I fail to see the reason why I'm on everyone's minds and lips. I'm not as bad as you make me out to be.*"

"Come again? Woman, I know you don't even believe that yourself." Etta Mae said.

"*Well, at least I was good to my husband, even though he was a big wuss. There once was something he wanted and he couldn't have, the man pouted and wouldn't eat for days! And do you know why?*"

"No, why?"

"*Naboth, our neighbor, the Jezreelite wouldn't sell him, and by him, I mean King Ahab, his land. That's why!*" Jezebel lamented. "*That land had been in this man's family for years. And you know he wasn't about to give his land up don't you? Would you?*"

"I know I wouldn't, and if anyone tried to take it, they would have a hell of a fight on their hands!" Tonika declared.

"*And guess why he wanted the land? Go on guess!*"

"I don't know . . . maybe to add to his possessions, maybe . . ." Etta Mae said.

"You're the one telling the story, so tell us why he wanted it." Tonika said.

"*Oh, I see you are the smart alec. Okay then here it is. Ahab that was his name you know . . .*"

"Yes, you told us. It's not like I—Tonika started to say.

"*He wanted the land to extend that little garden of his!*"

Jezebel yelled louder than she had intended.

"His garden, what's a king doing with a garden?" Tonika asked.

"And you're asking me? All I know is that he had one! Okay!"

The conversation went back and forth between Jezebel and Tonika. Etta Mae merely watched as each woman battled to outdo the other. Jezebel went on to further explain the situation that'd surrounded her husband's garden.

"I mean really, Tonika!" Jezebel threw both hands up in annoyance.

Tonika squirmed uneasily. She'd somehow gotten use to the unexpected presence of apparitions, but to be personally identified by them was something totally different.

"It was getting old I tell you, all that whining. So I said to the king, let's be real, is this the way a king supposed to act? Get up and eat, and cheer up! Ole Jez' got your back!"

"Yea, and I heard, or read rather, how you handled your business, girl!" Etta Mae finally chimed in.

"That's right, I was on it! As you say nowadays. You know it! Shucks half of the time my husband didn't even know how I did business! But, you know we women do have our ways remember?."

"I don't know Jezzie, I don't think anyone could be as conniving, and as manipulative as you, girlfriend. Like I told Tonika, you're queen of them all. I'd say you got us all beat."

"Well thanks for the compliment!"

Jezzie's high pitch laugher nearly pierced the ladies ear drums; they covered their ears.

"Uh hmm, to pick up where I left off . . ."

But before she could continue Etta Mae wanted to know about her dealings with Elijah, the Prophet.

"Wait, wait, wait, what I'd like to know is why did you threaten my man Elijah?"

"Elijah! You talking to me about that . . ." Jezebel shouted.

"Now why'd you bring that pest up?"

"I don't know, I just wondered why you pursued him like a hound dog."

"That man killed all my prophets! And when he messed with my livelihood, then he had to go! He'd just better be glad I didn't catch his pesky . . ."

"Yes, I know, but you did—

"Enough about that prophet already! Here's how it went down with Ahab, my husband!

"Okay, bring it down a tad; take a deep breath . . ." Etta Mae said soothingly.

Alright then, but just don't bring that name up again; promise?

"I won't or we won't, we promise." Etta Mae said.

Well, for starters, I forged Ahab's name on a letter accusing Naboth of a crime he never committed. I sealed it, sent it to the officials, and had two rascals speak against him in court."

"O! You were a sneaky something. And a controlling one at that!" Declared Tonika.

"Hee, hee, I know! Sometimes I even surprise myself!" Then in a more somber tone she added.

"If that's what you want to call it. It got the job done didn't it?"

"Oooh! She told you girlfriend; I tell you what, let's let her finish because I want to hear more."

"Thank you, mam." Jezebel made a mock bow to Etta Mae.

"Well needless to say, the man was found guilty and was stoned to death."

"O!Ouch!" Tonika proclaimed. "What a shame, that poor man."

"So, King Ahab got that land he wanted."

"Yes, but at what price?" Etta Mae asked. "That poor man was minding his own business and look what happened! That was so sad what you all did."

"Poor nothing, you do whatever it takes I always say! And besides, I just loved asserting my power."

Jezebel dismissed Etta Mae's display of sympathy with a wave of her hand.

"And I just bet you did."

Etta Mae always prided herself on being a fair judge of character, but out of all the villains in the Bible, this one topped the cake. She found herself disliking the conniving, manipulative, control freak of a female specimen, tremendously.

The women's dislike of her had no bearings on Jezebel. She hadn't gotten to be the most powerful woman in her day by caring what anyone thought. She had possessed unrivaled power, and that was all that mattered, and had made it a point to never sweat the small stuff.

"It is said you know that behind every great man, stands an even greater woman." Now am I right?"

"No, honey, I wouldn't say you were great; I would say you were more like trifling!" Tonika said. "And for the record, we don't stand behind our men, we stand beside them!"

"You tell her, Toni!" Etta Mae shouted proudly. But neither woman expected the venom that soon spewed forth.

"Oh, and you're standing beside yours, Tonika?"

A calculating laugh followed as Jezebel knowingly looked Tonika squarely in the eye.

"Ain't no use of going home . . . Joshie's packed his bags and gone." The wicked harpy sang.

"I am so sick of this!" Tonika exclaimed. She tearfully threw her hands up in surrender. "I'm sick of everybody, or everything knowing my damn business!"

"Well now that you know . . . may I finish without anymore interruptions, please?"

"Tonika, girl you're not making any friends here."

Etta Mae pulled her friend down within ear shot and whispered.

"So I would be careful if I were you. There's no telling what this thing may exact on us. So just be cool. Okay?"

"By all means, continue Jezebel, and Tonika don't interrupt her again. Okay?"

"Oh, alright, but you have to admit—

Etta Mae's look of disapproval cut the remark short.

Jezebel was satisfied with the reaction she'd gotten and proceeded with her tale. The most annoying human was finally silenced.

"*Now, where was I?*" The ghost figure began. "So, *things were going just super, until that pesky prophet Elijah came on the scene! But I even had him going too.*"

"Oh, so now she wants to talk Elijah!" Etta Mae said.

The sidekick wanted so badly to speak but was fortunately able to restrain herself.

"*But alas, even I had to pay to the piper. I had to heed the voice of God, and my fate wasn't a pretty* one. *I'm sure all of you've heard the story how I was thrown from a window by my two ungrateful servants.*

It just goes to show, you just-can't-get—good help. Those two old balless bastards listened to that rascal Jehu instead of listening to me."

Tonika jumped to her feet, unable to contain her excitement any further and let out a big cheer.

"Yeaaah! Go Jehu!" Then she said to Jezebel. "It served you right. You finally got your come-uppance!"

"*I'm glad my untimely demise made your day!*"

"Can you blame us?"

"*No, I don't put anything past you two . . . but to top it all off, this man Jehu . . . well his chariot runs over me after I was thrown over the balcony. Then those mangy dogs devoured my body. The only things left were my head and my feet!"*

"Eeewww! Gross!" Etta Mae and Tonika both said together.

"Well, it wasn't like you weren't warned. You received a prophecy "the dogs were going to lick your blood." Etta Mae commented.

"So I did, so I did, but all this beautiful body, can you believe it? Gone! You had to know it wasn't a pretty site."

"I'm sure it wasn't. I can't even imagine." Etta Mae said.

"Thanks for your sympathy."

"You're welcome, any time."

"If only I could turn back the hands of time! Why . . . why I would be a different woman!"

Jezebel lamented as she walked away from the two awe struck women. She returned to her position in the boutique, and transitioned once again into a lifeless mannequin.

The ladies sat for a while, and continued to stare at the store front.

"So the old bad girl got her due. Imagine being eaten by dogs, umph! They were right when they said the old girl's spirit still lives on, and we saw it for ourselves today. So it is definitely true."

"Ya think! Now don't you go buying any of her underwear because I wouldn't be able to handle another of her kind."

"Who're you telling? None of that Chantilly lace is touching any of this!"

"And who have you been talking to that you know about her spirit?"

"What do you mean?"

"You sounded as if you knew something about her before I told you."

"Oh, I ran into Sister Edna Brown a few days ago."

"Motor-mouth Edna? Come on let's get out of here, I'm kind of drained. Aren't you?"

The two ladies picked up their purses and started for the exit.

"Edna's always humming, *Blessed Assurance, Jesus in mine* every Sunday. I found myself humming it this morning."

"She does have a way of getting to you. She always sits in the third row on the left side of the church, and her mouth is always going."

The women walked faster than usual. They weren't interested in having another encounter. Three were enough for the day.

"God bless her; if you ever ask how she's doing, have some time on your hand, because for an hour or so you'll have to hear her testimony."

"What's her favorite line . . ." Lord, I'm blessed and highly favored."

Hysterical laughter carried the two into the welcoming sunlight. They were elated to finally escape the dark and unearthly atmosphere inside the mall.

"Miss Edna broke it down to me child, she even gave me a page from let's see; um, um, hum, hum, hum. Oh! Here it is . . . something she got off the web about Jezebel in Our Society by this Albatrus man."

Tonika pulled the piece of paper from her purse and began to read the contents.

"Listen to what it says."

"The Jezebel spirit is born of witchcraft and rebellion. This demon is one of the most common spirits in operation today, both in the church and in the world, and it is a powerful enemy of the body of Christ. She operates freely on sincere believers whose hearts are for God individually, and has also attained positions of power as powers and principalities within the Church. This spirit establishes its stronghold primarily in women; however, many men have been victimized by it as well, where it functions as a "controlling" spirit.

The spirit of Jezebel is behind the daughter of Democracy, i. e. Feminism. The Spirit of Jezebel is basically a controlling spirit working through the lust of the flesh, and the lust of the eyes, and the pride of life. It has, in general, two aims:

To gain identity, glory, recognition, power, and satisfy the need for the "praises of men". This is a consequence of the desire for love and self-worth focused on SELF.

"Now that's deep." Etta Mae said.

Tonika continued reading, but paused long enough to agree.

"Now, ain't it though?"

Jezebel was and is a political figure and uses spiritual control and manipulation to exert influence.

"Ummph, I'm sure glad Edna enlightened you, now you have something to top what she knows."

"You're right about that, but who'd believe it? Wait, there's more."

Once under this delusionary spirit, she takes them captive, disguises herself as the spirit of God, and allows false prophecy, idolatry and worldly practices to flourish."

"I'll stop right there, because after reading this, girlfriend . . . with what we just encountered I'd say we were too up close, and too personal for my taste."

"I know that's right, now I'm with you there." Etta Mae agreed. "I can't get away from here fast enough!"

Tonika folded the slip of paper and slid it back inside her purse.

"I think we should be glad we got out of there with our heads!"

The women moved on with a sense of urgency. The stifling heat inside the car soon dissipated with welcoming coolness.

Etta Mae backed the car out of the parking stall and aimed it towards the busy freeway.

The day's paranormal activity bounced around in their heads. A ringing cell phone broke the silence, which brought about a frantic search.

"That's mine." Etta Mae said. She maneuvered the car with one hand.

"Hello? Cyndi, baby! How're you doing, honey? . . . That's good . . . I-I'm doing okay, now that I'm where it's cool . . . Uh, huh, uh, huh. Uh-huh, uh-huh."

"This is Cyndi, my baby sister."

Etta Mae listened while mouthing to her passenger.

"Girl, I haven't heard from you since . . . how was Hawaii? Great! Janet and Geoffrey said they enjoyed you . . . yes, they called last Sunday. Donnie told you I was out shopping? Uh-huh, I bet he did . . . well actually we're on our way home and should be there in about ten to fifteen minutes . . . No, Dee's not with me. Well, when I left she was taking a nap. Did Donnie say she wasn't there? Humph, then I couldn't tell you where she is. But let me ask you this . . . do you know what's going on with our sister? Uh huh . . . no, she hasn't told me enough to know what's really going on. She begins to and then she stops like it's too much to even talk about. Then she'll get into her Delilah Collins mode. *Ha, ha, ha, ha.* yes, you know our sister. Yes . . . that's right. But I do know it's got something to do with her husband though. Oh, you did? Ooh, girl that's something."

Etta Mae stole a look at her passenger, and shrugged her shoulders. She had a surprised look on her face.

"W-well, I tell you what, I'll call you back when I get home. I had an experience last night too. Did He show you anything else?

Oh, okay . . . I see. Okay, sweetie, yeah, uh-huh, uh huh, I'll talk to you later. Love you too! Smooches! Bye now. Okay, I'll tell her baby, bye bye now."

"Cynthia even knows there's something going on with our sister."

"How, what does she know?"

"She said that she'd had a vision of our sister boarding a plane to come to me."

"Oh! Is Cynthia a psychic or something?"

"Well, she is deeply rooted. She studied theology and all, so I don't doubt that she hasn't been given a spiritual gift or two. God does reward those who diligently seek Him you know."

"Then that would explain it, she could have the gift of knowledge."

"Yep, she could at that."

"After everything we've been through today, nothing surprises me."

Etta Mae raised her hand to heaven and prayed.

"Lord! Whatever you are doing right now . . . don't do it without me! *Please*, don't do it without me. Amen and amen!"

"Oh, oh, and Lord, don't forget about me, Tonika please!"

The two women fell silent once again. The drone of the car's tires reverberated in a rhythmic sound.

"I tested HIV positive!"

The dreaded words exploded out of Tonika's mouth like Mount St. Helen's eruption.

She felt surprisingly relieved. The pent up stress was finally resolved. The secret that had sat in the pit of her stomach like a ton of bricks was finally out.

However, she was not prepared for the flood of hot blinding

tears that cascaded down her face. The liberated woman sobbed uncontrollably, gulping air in between trembles.

"Toni! Are you alright?" Etta Mae asked, genuinely concerned.

She pulled the car over into a vacant parking lot, suddenly needing to console her dear friend. Etta Mae put the car into park but allowed the engine to run the air conditioner for their comfort.

"Oh Toni, I'm so sorry, I didn't know."

"I-I."

The words Tonika wanted to utter couldn't find their way past the knot in her throat, she cried even more. "Don't talk, just let me hold you."

Etta Mae gathered her stricken friend in her arms and offered what comfort she was able to give.

How had this happened? Never in her wildest dreams could she ever imagine someone so close to her find themselves in such a dilemma.

The comforting companion soon realized the amount of fortitude her friend had to have possessed to silently bare a burden of such magnitude. She would never, ever under any circumstances underestimate her again.

Not once had she ever let on that her very existence was in jeopardy. Perhaps sharing the Gospel with her through the years had solidified her faith for sure.

"So, where to from here girlie?" Etta Mae somberly asked. "You have to find Josh and tell him, you know."

"Yes, I know." Tonika quietly said, without lifting her head. "Who knew just one little letter from a doctor could destroy your whole world."

She hadn't had any symptoms. According to the letter, she may've had it for quite some time, but weren't aware of it.

Clinical latent infection typically lasts 8 to 10 years. The letter had read. A few people stay in this stage even longer, but others progress to a more-severe disease much sooner.

After she read that statement she knew her husband's extra marital affair couldn't possibly be the culprit, unless, it hadn't been his first.

In any case, she reasoned that she had been true to her marriage vows. The decision to text Josh, asking him to meet her at home was the next step.

"Who're you calling or texting rather?"

"I'm texting Josh to see if he would meet me at home. We didn't do much talking before, but maybe we can come to some resolution today."

Tonika looked at her best friend and solemnly asked. "Pray for me Etta Mae, please."

"Girl! You know I got you!"

Etta Mae reached over to take hold of her friend's hand.

"When do you go back to the doctor?"

"On Monday, I have an appointment for 10:00." Tonika sent the text to Josh. "There! It's done, now let's see what happens."

"Did you ask him any questions when you talked with him?" Etta Mae wanted to know. "And by the way, when did you find out, and why haven't you told me before now?"

"Slow your roll!" Tonika managed to say with a smile. "And no, we didn't talk . . . we just yelled at each other. I've just been so upset with finding that damn note—

"Tonika! How could something like that slip your mind? Do you know this ain't anything to play with?"

"Damn it, Etta Mae! Who goes to have your iron level checked and expect to hear you're HIV positive? And besides I haven't even come to grips with it myself."

"Tonika, wait a minute . . . you had a transfusion some years ago, didn't you?"

"Yes, when Adrika—

"That's it! Tonika! That could be it!" Etta Mae said excitedly.

"I doubt it . . . And as far as that goes, it's not exactly like the opportunity has presented itself. You were either busy with Donnie, your sister, and not to mention with all those visitations today."

"What about the drive to the mall? You could've told me then."

"Well, to be truthful friend, with something such as this, you don't know who to tell. Deep down, I knew you would be there for me and all, but sometimes even your friends turn on you out of fear. I'm sorry I didn't trust you enough to be there for me."

Etta Mae was truly concerned with her friend's well-being and was kind of pained she hadn't shared it with her.

It now made sense why their afternoon excursion was anything but jovial. But, in any case, she knew it would certainly benefit Tonika to look into the matter of the transfusion.

Tonika continued to talk but her cohort's mind was too deep in thought to hear what she said.

"I know we share a lot . . . but this is something that I wanted to discuss with my . . ." She stopped short of saying my husband, but her mouth was unable to form the words.

Tonika didn't even know if there would be a marriage after last night. This was unfortunate, because she really did believe in the sanctity of it. But, alas it does take two to make it work.

"I-I just wanted to discuss it with Josh first." She finally said. "And I know it's going to be hard, but there is light at the end of the tunnel. I just have to keep going."

"W-what? I'm sorry Toni . . . what were you saying? My mind—

"I was saying . . . never mind." Tonika began. "I'll discuss everything with you later."

Silence enveloped the car once again. As they neared home, rampant thoughts flickered through each of their minds.

Chapter Seventeen

"Now there you go again . . ." Damian said, now feeling a bit uneasy while conspicuously inspecting every darkened corner of the spacious living room.

"Okay, suit yourself, but I wouldn't put it past him. I'm through being surprised."

Suddenly, an eerie sound was heard at the utterance of Donnie's last words. Eve appeared in the same manner she had earlier.

"Hot damn!" Damien yelped. "Man! Is this what, or who you were trying to warn me about?"

He couldn't keep his knees from knocking with fear.

"Adam! Adam honey, where are you?"

Donnie was now familiar with the phantom figure. This time, no uncontrollable bodily functions occurred.

"Say guys . . . you haven't seen a big, tall black man wearing animal skin, have you? He's supposed to be here by now."

Then Eve pointedly addressed Donnie.

"Donnie, I see you're completely dry for a change."

The startled man could fill the blood rush to his face from the embarrassment of Eve's callous remark. He lowered his head and quietly answered.

"No, I-I haven't seen Adam."

"*Humph . . . I wonder what's keeping him.*"

Even though the unexpected shock of Eve's sudden appearance was waning, Donnie focused his attention on the apparition's purpose for visiting his home . . . yet again.

"And you're here *be-cause?*"

"*Now, I know you know this is not my first visit to your humble abode, so why did you ask that question?*"

"Yes, you're correct." The unintentional host stated. "And you're in my home again because . . . ?"

Eve nonchalantly strolled over to the mahogany sofa table, leaving the perplexed host to wonder if she'd heard his question.

She smiled at the familiar surroundings and lovingly picked up a photo of the home's occupants they had taken during a Caribbean cruise the year before.

"*Hmmm . . . nice picture.*"

She carefully returned it to the array of photos on the table and turned back to the gentlemen with a devilish look in her eye.

"*I saw you this morning while I was speaking with your wife and her friend . . . what's her name?*"

"Tonika" Donnie inserted. Eve was slightly amused.

"*So you really do know how to pronounce her given name.*"

She'd long since dismissed her unpleasant opinion of the unbridled character she'd had the unfortunate pleasure of meeting.

"*You know guys, I couldn't help but over hear your conversation a while ago. So what exactly did you mean by asking . . . did Adam ask God for that woman?*"

"You mean you heard that?" Damien scratched his head in wonderment. "Damn! What don't you hear?"

"*You sound like my husband.*" Eve said. "And *you do know your boy told God, "It was that woman you gave me."* Eve shucked her teeth and turned away again. *"You men are all alike, chips off the old block!"*

Neither of the gentleman cared for her callous statement. Donnie uttered a well-defined expletive.

"Oh, hell no! Now you're wrong on that one Miss Evie."

Damien decided to interject a bit of biblical fact.

"Hel-lo, news flash!" He exclaimed.

The attention grabber stopped the grand matron in her tracks.

"Woman! Your reputation has preceded you for eons. I don't have to tell you that Adam wasn't the only one that blamed you."

Eve was jolted out of her stupor. The younger of the men now held her attention, even though she disliked what he'd said.

"Go on . . . I'm waiting to hear." She folded her arms in defiance.

"The Apostle Paul said in 1Timothy 2:14 Adam wasn't the one deceived. He said it was you . . . and that you had become a sinner." Damien felt bolder by the minute.

"Saul-Paul had his nerves, but what can I say?" Eve gave Damian the once over. *"And you can talk!"*

She stepped forward until she was toe to toe with her accuser.

"So what's your excuse for the life you lead? At least I was truthful to my man! And besides he wasn't complete without me."

"If you say so . . ." It took Damien a moment to recoup from the shock of the apparition's knowledge of his antics.

"Well, I do say so!"

Donnie was amused at the skirmish unfolding before his eyes.

"I guess my man looked so pitiful that our compassionate Father put my baby to sleep and . . . ta da!"

"And I don't suppose your man ever missed that rib."

Donnie playfully shoved Damien in the ribs with an elbow. Eve chose to ignore it.

"Speaking of my short rib, you sure you haven't seen him?"

"Seen him? I can't even believe I'm seeing you!" Donnie responded.

"Where did you come from anyways? You were already here with my wife, so why the return visit?"

"Yes, I was."

"Why do you people, I mean you ghosts keep popping up in my house? And aren't you supposed to be in Heaven somewhere?"

"Yikes!"

Damian jumped about four feet in the air. The appearance of another unimaginable creature had suddenly manifested out of nowhere.

The man called Adam stood a towering six feet. His chiseled body gleamed like the finest polished black onyx. The shiny onyx head was supported by a neck the size of a young oak.

Piercing eyes encased in sockets set far apart under a protruding brow searched the unfamiliar surroundings. A strong jaw and a narrowed nose with flaring nostrils completed the handsome being.

His physique boasted of a flat stomach etched in a six pack, well defined with deep crevices between each muscle. Long, sculptured arms that extended well below mid-thigh hung from broad, muscular shoulders.

Adam sported a hairy animal loin cloth that was connected from front to back by a strong black cord. Massive thighs and bulging calves supported his massive frame.

Admittedly, the two male humans were dwarfed in dimensions in comparison to the sculpted specimen that stood before them.

"Oh, there you are . . . don't ever leave me like that again." Eve said, cooing in a seductive voice. *"You know I almost always get into trouble when you're not with me."*

"*Now, that you do!*" Adam said in a matter of fact manner. "*You weren't supposed to come here without me!*"

"*Oh, babe, you never could keep up with me, now could you.*"

Eve playfully declared, thrilled to be reunited with her Adam once again.

"*You have got to quit doing that!*" Adam admonished in a thundering voice full of concern.

"*I'm sorry . . . but I have to tell you this is not my first visit here.*" Eve said, speaking with false humility, she lowered her head.

"*You mean you've been here before now?*" Adam asked.

Yes, I met Etta Mae, this man's wife." She said pointing to Donnie. "*And her snooty best friend this morning. Can't say I liked them much either, especially the one called To-To, something or other.*"

"To-ni-ka!" Donnie and Damian both chimed in.

"*Okay al-ready! To-ni-ka!*"

"*Don't let them get the best of you, babe.*" Adam tweaked his wife's nose and said softly. "*That's just homo sapiens for you.*"

Eve took a hold of Adam's hand and rubbed it against her cheek.

"*Did you know they're still mad at me for causing women to go through the pain of childbirth? I hope they know I was the first to suffer! So why are they complaining!*"

The two are so engrossed with one another, and so into their conversation that everyone else was temporarily forgotten.

The whole scenario was so absurd and comical that the two hombres shared a laugh.

"*Yep,*" Adam said to the men. "*Like I'm sure these fellows are mad at me for causing them to break a sweat just to make a living. What did the Word say? "If a man doesn't work, he doesn't eat?"*"

"Well, I don't sweat when I'm working." Damien said with his voice edged with pride. "I barely push a pencil, or better yet, strike a few keys on a keypad."

"No need to justify why you don't sweat, my brother." Donnie shook his head. "I only sweat when I'm on the golf course, myself."

"Well, I am so happy for you two, apparently I didn't mess things up too badly!"

Once again, Adam felt it necessary to reprimand his wife for her disappearing act.

"I really wish you would stay put, you know what happened the last time you went exploring."

"Do I remember . . . how could I forget? Eve said thoughtfully. She took a few steps back and sauntered over to the window.

"But you do know it was not my fault. My mind wasn't even on . . ."

Adam walked over to where his Wife stood.

"No, it was all my fault; no one put a rock to my head, if that's what you mean."

"Apology accepted." Eve turned to embrace her love. *"But I do have to tell you that I was pretty upset with you for saying what you said. I even called you a wimp to the ladies today. Sorry."*

"Apology accepted."

Donnie and Damian looked on in bewilderment. If anyone had told them a situation such as this would come up, they would have bet on the Mega Millions. The chances were just that slim.

Yet, here was the first Adam and the first woman in his living room.

"Somebody, please pinch me." Donnie whispered under his breath.

Damian was only too glad to oblige, and reached over to do just that, but was stopped in his tracks with the coldest stare.

They both turned their attention again to the scene being played out in the room.

"*But you do know it wasn't until you bit the fruit that everything fell apart!*" Eve told Adam.

"Ah excuse me, 'scuse me." Donnie said. He walked over to the sparring couple. "But what are you two doing? And then too, why're you acting like we're not even in the room?"

He was disenchanted with the whole fiasco and the tirade continued.

"Miss 'Thang' here just waltzes up in my house like it belongs to her! And then you pop up from out of nowhere! There ought to be a law!"

"*It is all you human's fault.* Adam retorted.

"Oh, here we go." Donnie blurted. "The old blame game."

"*Didn't God say that man was not to meddle with the spirit world or practice magic or sorcery?*"

Adam drove home his point by driving his index finger repeatedly into Donnie's chest.

"*But no, as usual, like any other law, you humans find a way to break them all at the drop of a hat.*"

Donnie backed away from the unwanted contact and rubbed the invaded spot.

"*Ah honey . . . honey, I-I already covered that same topic with the women earlier, so . . .*" Eve told her husband. "*So they already know who's to blame.*"

"I can't believe you two!" Donnie shouted. "And we don't know jack! So you got me pegged wrong dude!"

"I don't go anywhere looking for any ghosts! It's those geeks on television that goes into haunted homes and hotels looking for 'em"

"And me neither." Damian quickly added. "I don't even watch ghost movies let alone looking for them."

"Yeah and how can you talk about anyone breaking laws anyway when you clearly . . ." Donnie boldly asked.

"*Okay . . . you got me there, dude.*" Adam said. "*And I know you two bro-thas don't, because the two of you are . . . shall we say, quite timid.* The first man laughed a roaring laugh. "*Two big scaredy cats!*"

"I got your scaredy cat." Damien, defiantly shouted. "You're a ghost and I'm talking to you, aren't I!"

"*Boo!*" Adam jovially shouted. "*I'm a ghost and I just spooked you!*" He laughed once again.

"Let me out of here . . . all this shit is crazy!"

Damien brushed past Donnie only to be grabbed by Adam.

"*Oh, no you don't Brotha-Man! I came here especially for you.*"

"What did you say? You came for me . . . why, what did I do?"

"*I just wanted to tell you that your heavenly Father is not pleased with the way your life is going. In fact, He's not particularly pleased with the way the whole world has gone. Unfortunately, dare I say, due to yours truly.*"

Both Donnie and Eve watched closely. Adam remained standing as Damien, sat down on the couch. He felt as if the wind had been knocked out of him.

"You got that right! You were weak, man! You should have seen through that wily old serpent." Donnie went over and joined the two.

"*It's like I just told my wife, I take full responsibility for my actions.*" Adam replied. "*I messed up, so you're all going to hell in a hand basket!*"

"Oh, no we're not!" Damian exclaimed. He jumped up from his seat.

"We're not because of what the last Adam did. And those of us that believe on Him are wondrously redeemed. Glory to God!"

There was an instant look of shock on everyone's face, but they listened intently.

"You're the first Adam, but God's son, Jesus Christ is the last Adam. And He came to save us all, including you two. Hallelujah anyhow!"

"Well . . . aren't you your father's son." Adam looked at the preaching human with amusement. *"You preach just like him."*

"Look at you! I didn't know you had it in you, brother!" Donnie said, pleasantly surprised at the young man's outburst.

"And like Rev. D. here said, if I'm not mistaken, because of Jesus, you and your girl here were even redeemed."

Adam thought perhaps he may have overestimated the situation, and looked thoughtfully at the two men.

"True, true, I'm forever grateful to Him and I thanked Christ personally when He came to paradise after His death."

He quieted himself by just thinking about the enormous price the Savior had paid for mankind. Then he perked up once again.

"You talk about something bright! Oo-wee! There we were on the comfort side of Hades, in Paradise, when all of a sudden, a beam of light brighter than the sun lit up the whole place. It was so bright it even lit up hell, the tormented side."

"What is the tormented side?" Damien asked with concern. "Is hell divided or something with a good and a bad side?"

"It's hard to believe, isn't it?" Adam answered. *"And yes, it was, to answer your question, but not anymore."*

Thinking more on the matter, Adam addressed Damien with a question.

"Wait a minute . . . you were a PK. So, if either of you two would know about hell, it should be you. Your father preached on Luke 16:19-

31 one Sunday morning on November 16, 1988, but of course as usual, you were nodding off."

"Like I remember every sermon my dad ever preached!" Damien shouted. "Apparently that's where you come in."

Adam chose not to respond to Damien's outburst, but continued to tell about Jesus' stay in Hades.

"So . . . for a brief moment in time, hell was lit up! We even got to look in on the darkness over there, and what a horror to behold. Demons squirmed and wiggled and hid their ugly faces. And the tormented people . . . . O, my Lord! Of course, hell couldn't help but be lit, because wherever He is darkness has to flee! Can I get an Amen?"

"Amen!"

His wife shouted from across the room.

"Thanks babe. I tell you, from what I could see over there, you don't want to go to that place. It is hor-ri-ble! I pity the fool!"

Donnie looked at Damien, then back to Adam and anxiously proclaimed.

"You see, I told you, I told you! My God will do anything to keep us from that place. He didn't build it for us anyway. It was only meant for Satan and his imps!"

Donnie stood and paced the floor, unable to bridle the excitement he felt at this jubilation.

"Damian, my friend," he said, "have you ever heard of the living Bible? Well here it stands, right before our very eyes!"

Damien, with a hung head was speechless. He stuck his hands between his legs and sat quietly.

"Adam!" Donnie continued. "Just tell me you're not really here!"

Everything was too unbelievable.

"I know what, I'm dreaming and when I wake up, neither one of you will be here, including old Double D."

He slapped his face with a resounding smack.

"Damn!" He said, recoiling from the sting. "That hurt! And all of you are still here!"

The befuddled man also took his seat. "That Etta Mae Smith started all this. Now she's nowhere around."

"No, you're not dreaming."

Adam smiled unabashedly over the discomfort their presence caused the two gentlemen.

"And yes, I'm, that is, we really are here."

He drew his woman closer to the inner circle.

"Do you realize that the lies of Satan are behind all the drama that has been going on in your life? Eve said. "And your father knows exactly what you're up to. You have been led astray."

"You know my dad!" Damien asked, astonished.

Know him? If it weren't for his request to come and deliver you, we wouldn't be here." Adam assured Damien.

"Deliver me, deliver me from what?"

"All I'm saying is that what you're going through is all due to a deceptive spirit. And the Jezebel spirits along with their friends are behind it all.

They are all controlling, deceitful, as well as, lying spirits that are totally against anything that has been ordained as righteous."

"You're speaking gibberish . . . who or what are you talking about?" Damien asked, confused. Donnie looked on.

"Let me break it down for you, brotha. The spirit of deception and his buddy, that old slimy perverted spirit is hard at work today. "Your world is Sodom and Gomorrah, all over again!" Eve declared.

Damian jumped up, clasped his head in his hands and shouted.

"Spare me please! Now, it's coming from all sides; first Donnie and now you two! A damn spirit! No, two spirits!" He nervously paced the floor.

"I'm talking to two spirits! Somebody, please shoot me."

"Damian!" Eve said, taking him by the hand and holding it in hers.

"Sweetie, you would do well to listen! Even I know that the sin that serpent of a devil brought into the world was to confuse all of mankind about their purpose in life."

"Wait a minute," Donnie said, "I have one question."

"And what is your question?" The power couple asked.

"Why do you two talk like us? Honey this and honey' that! Aren't you supposed to talk bibley-gook, the thees and the thous?"

"Hey, yeah, you're right!" Damien said in agreement. "They sound like they're from the 21st century."

"Ahem!" Eve cleared her throat. *"Allow me, please babe . . . Guys, you see we travel from century to century, and we take on the persona of the era we land in."*

The befuddled gentlemen shook their heads in recognition.

"Donnie you seem to be doing pretty good." Adam said. *"But, I have to tell you . . . there is one thing your Maker has against you."*

"And that being?" Donnie sarcastically inquired.

"Thou shall have no other gods before Me!" Sound familiar? Donnie, have you been golfing lately my good man?"

Donnie swallowed past a big lump in his throat.

"Y-Yes, I was out there today and on my game. Hey . . . wait a minute! I go to church, if that's what you're implying."

The spirit couple looked on in amusement. Donnie continued to justify his actions or lack thereof.

"I just didn't go Sunday, because we had a golf tour-na . . . ment. He paused before saying softly.

"And besides, you can't stay around Etta Mae Smith, and the Word not rub off on you."

"Do you know what Donnie?" Eve asked.

"What Miss Eve."

"Your wife doesn't actually know where your stance is when it comes to the Father. She does know that you occasionally read your Bible, but you never voice your stand, or add anything when and if you go to Wednesday night Bible study.

May I remind you, of what Jesus said in Revelation 3:1 "I know your deeds; you have a reputation of being alive, but you are dead! Wake up!"

"Well, I dare say, it ain't none of her business!"

Donnie was upset by the fact that he had to face himself, his soul had been laid bare.

It didn't help to realize he'd stood in judgment pretty much a part of the day on Damien's life, but hadn't bothered to examine his own. However, still in defiance, he chose to put on a brave front.

"That's between me and my God. I-I just don't let the old girl know it, but I do listen when she's quoting scriptures." He said in his defense. "Plus the fact that she drags me to church."

Donnie tried to make light of his statement, but the humor wasn't shared by the occupants in the room.

"Just kidding, my wife, in no form or fashion has to drag me to the house of God. Actually, I look forward to going, when I know Pastor Hershel is preaching that is."

He nervously laughed again, and received the same reaction. Finally Eve said.

"Just remember my dear fellow; it is not your wife that you must answer to, but the One who called you lukewarm. And, believe me He will spew you out of His mouth! In other words, the Lord is saying; "Don't play with Me!"

"Oh, you guys are wrong! That scripture wasn't talking about me! Now, you're wrong on that one."

"Case in point!" Damien exclaimed. "Now let's get back to me! The one you appear to know quite a bit about. It seems to me; you ought to be minding your own business."

Well, like I said, Jesus redeemed me, and He can do the same thing for you, my son. Adam addressed Damien directly. *"All you have to do is to "confess with your mouth, and believe in your heart that He is Lord."*

"How're you going to fix your mouth?" Damien shouted. "You see! If you've been watching me as you said, then you would know that I already did just that; at a young age!"

"Did I not say that I had been watching you for a lifetime? How then can you say, I do not know you?" Adam relentlessly quizzed Damien. *"I know when you made your first childlike confession, unfortunately, so does the old adversary. That is why he went after you because of the plan for your life. I came for such a time as this."*

"I don't know why you came here. It's not like you can do anything to save me. Besides, I don't need you to remind me of anything."

The argument between the two was beginning to escalate. Damien didn't care to be reminded of his short comings in the spiritual department and had become resentful of the fact that he was being confronted. Adam, however, meant to deliver on his assignment.

"I have to do, what I have to do."

Now aren't you suddenly the Holy One!"

"No . . . If I was the Holy One you wouldn't be talking smack; you'd be on your knees repenting."

"Oh, so you're here to put a G.A.G. order on me." Damien said.

Puzzled faces stared back at him. "God's Amazing Grace!" He yelled. "Geez!"

"No, since I'm not the Holy One of Israel I can't do that, only He was sent for that purpose."

Laying all humor aside, Adam gave it to Damien with both guns blazing.

"I'm merely on assignment. I know what it's like to think you've gotten away with tomfoolery, but God knew, and still knows. Nothing is hidden from Him. He's all seeing and all knowing."

Uh, I believe that's called, Omniscient. H-he's omniscient." Donnie quickly interjected. Only to be silenced by the cold stares.

"And I tell you something else." The first human said. *"It's sad to say that even my first son Cain, who did the unthinkable by murdering his own brother was stupid enough to believe that he could hide the murder from God. But let it be known that everyone's actions have consequences; good or bad.*

My own son allowed his jealousy to turn to anger, then to hate. Even when Abel's blood cried out to God from the ground, to avenge him, your God and my God, had enough love and compassion for the one who took his own brother's life, to place a mark on the murderer's forehead, lest anyone should do him harm."

Eve listened intently, while her husband told of their most heartbreaking moment. All of the tears she had shed over the plight of her two sons had fallen to the cursed earth. Her tears had watered the thorns and the thistles that had sprung up.

"Now bear with me here." Adam droned on. *"The earth then, has become saturated with the blood of your brothers ever since. We're sorry . . . and we apologize wholeheartedly. That same murderous spirit that caused the death of our beloved son is privy to do the same to your sons and daughters today."*

Eve couldn't take it any longer. She knew her tears had become the forerunner of the many tears mothers would shed through eons to come.

"Look at what is happening every day in your world; blood is constantly spilled, brother killing brother. And all that blood cries out to the Creator each time the earth opens its mouth to receive it.

Mothers are weeping just as I wept that day in the field. Sadly, they will continue to weep."

Adam went over to console his grieving wife. Her small stature was over shadowed as he enveloped her in a warm embrace.

"Its okay, the Lord gave us other sons and daughters to share our love. One by which His only begotten son would bear lineage, so all was not lost. Now dry your tears, we're nearly done here anyway. Okay?"

"Okay . . . but you know what?" Eve said with a smile.

"What's that dear?"

"When the Father said my seed would crush the head of the serpent, I-I thought He meant it would be our son Cain." She began to sob once again.

"I know you did, I know you did; there, there, now. We eventually got it right."

The captive audience hadn't been able to utter a word. They were so engrossed in the compelling drama being played out. Adam soon returned to the task at hand.

"Your neighborhood gang doesn't realize it, but they're nothing but mere puppets in the hands of the enemy. In the mist of every known gang are representatives of Satan, mainly the spirit of coercion. It compels one to do an act, or to make a choice they hadn't planned to do. It's a 'voice in your head' so to speak. This spirit causes minds to serve evil. Consequently the more they're susceptible to this spirit, the greater the evil they will accomplish.

The gangs will continue to cause death and destruction, because no one can seem to deliver them. At this very moment, your nation is crying over a poor young man's spilled blood, whose life was taken by someone who listened to the voice of the enemy."

"Oh, I feel for all those mothers." Eve interjected. *"Their tears are watering the earthlike mine. The whole nation feels the pain.*

It's like Jeremiah 31:15 says; "A voice is heard in Ramah, mourning and great weeping, Rachel weeping for her children and refusing to be comforted, because her children are no more."

She walked away from the men and stood at the window again, sadly looking out.

"I-I know what you're saying is true." Damien said. "And . . . I heartedly repent of my misdoings. It even grieves me to think about them."

Everyone in the room was deeply touched. A sole tear even cascaded down Donnie's face.

Adam's preaching had ignited such a flame in the remorseful young man's heart, that after suffering deep conviction Damien knelt down and prayed a soul wrenching prayer of repentance.

"O, Lord, I ask you to come into my heart, and renew my mind and my spirit. Heavenly Father, I want the mind of Christ from this day forward; a mind that will love, obey, and do Your Will. Lord, I renounce Satan and all he stands for. I renounce the spirit of perversion, and the spirit of false pride that had me in its grips far too long.

I believe you are the Son of the Living God, and you died for my sins. Lord, your Word says; "though my sins are of crimson," Lord I know your blood can wash them white as snow. Wash me Lord, cleanse me. I want my life to belong solely to you. Lord, I am no longer who man says I am, but I am who you say I am; a son of the Most High God. I surrender my all to you. I have prayed this prayer in the Name of your Son, Jesus the Christ. Amen."

As he knelt there he was enveloped with a sense of peace, love and joy. Damien had never felt so much love. He celebrated by jumping to his feet and shouting aloud.

"Praise the Lord! I have been set free!"

Everyone in the room rejoiced. He ran over to Donnie and began to explain his feelings.

"I truthfully thought everything was acceptable in a no holds barred society, so, I gave into the forbidden desires. And I justified it by telling myself I wasn't alone in my sordid acts.

Everyone is so proud of being the way they are." He said forlornly.

"They all seemed to proudly shout out their hidden secrets with pride."

"Life does have a way of deceiving you and bogging you down."

Donnie truly empathized with the young man's plight.

"You're right." Adam said in agreement. *"But, can I tell you the real reason they're all coming out? Their coming out is not of their own choosing, but, it's the 'omniscient one' pulling the covers back. That perverted spirit operated in secrecy far too long; it's now exposed."*

"If that's the case, then why do people gladly admit their preferences?"

"Deceit can no longer hide its ugly head. You read in the Scriptures "everything done in the dark will come to light." If God said it, then it has to come to pass."

"You got that right!" Eve chimed in. *"You can't pull anything over on the 'Big Guy.' I don't know just how long it's going to take you people to realize that! Just like me and Adam, we thought we were being slick . . . remember babe, when we hid."*

"Eve, honey . . . we've already covered that, but yes, I do remember. Oh, how I remember."

"Sorry babe, I just can't forget. But do carry on, by all means."

"Thank you; And Donnie . . . to answer your question, the sad thing is, once those perverted spirits have been revealed, a false sense of pride takes over; another trick of the enemy, the 'spirit of pride. And so instead of asking for deliverance, mankind rejoices in their deception.

But, the Father does not approve of the vigilante attitude man has acquired. The only thing He wants mankind to do is to love unconditionally. No matter what their takes are in life; we're all His children."

"Amen to that!" Donnie shouted. "So we don't need to be killing, mutilating or bashing anyone over the head for their life's choices. God does not need our help."

"Here, here!" Damien said.

"Now take my man here." Donnie said. "He grew up in the church!"

"Just where're you going with this?"

"I was just—

"Listen, I don't need you to stand in judgment of me!" Damien angrily shouted. "You don't know what I went through!"

Flashbacks of his life, his boyhood rape, had been particularly running through his head during the whole discussion.

"Oo! Why so much anger?" Donnie tauntingly asked.

"You know nothing is as it seems. How do you know I wasn't turned out at church, huh? Man! The church can't . . ."

"He's right you know." Adam watched the play by play drama and solemnly said.

"Those very spirits can and do live at the church. Your children are not even safe. Now that act alone . . . Well, the Father said "it is better a 'mill stone' was tied around their necks than to harm his little ones.

All one has to do is read today's headlines, to know no one is exempt. Those powerful spirits, or I should say, principalities, the generals, will take down the most fire preaching, oil slinging, preacher in the pulpit, if they're not careful."

"But, listen gentlemen our time is up here. I believe I've accomplished what I was sent here to do. So I just wanted to leave both of you with this thought.

And that is; God loves you no matter what you do or say. He can't help but love you, because He is love.

And Damien, just to let you know, He heard you when you made your confession in your father's church. I just come to help that confession burn bright in your heart once again.

So that you may experience His Holy Spirit strengthening you, in order that the fruit of the spirit, self-control may over shadow your carnal mind.

Damien, my God, and your God loves you so much that I personally came to speak you into your destiny; to preach His Holy Word.

Now, go with hope in your heart, and peace in your spirit. And begin to declare the victory of your deliverance over every area in your life, where ever you may feel defeated. And I would say, at the moment that would be your marriage."

Adam placed his hand on the weeping convert's shoulder before offering the last piece of encouragement.

"But take heart my friend; God has already worked it out!"

Then offering his arm, Adam turned to his wife. "And now my love . . . shall we?"

She readily grasped his arm, and they both walked off into oblivion.

"Always remember my noble friends . . ." Deliverance is always available to you!"

"Wow! Who could say anything after that?" Damien thought. The two of them sat as if frozen in time.

Finally, Damien rose from his seat and offered his hand to Donnie.

"I think I'll head back to the hotel."

The perplexed host accepted the extended hand and stood up.

"Alright, dude."

Donnie was able to say despite the churning in his stomach. The two finished their handshake with a series of hand daps.

"We've been through a lot these past few hours, so I guess that makes us 'bosom buddies' so to speak."

"And I know I have a lot to think on, but I do want to thank you for finally letting me in . . . Brotha-Man!"

Laughter was the order of the moment as they recalled the earlier fiasco.

"Sorry for the scare."

Donnie grabbed and hugged the burden-lifted young man and followed with a sound pat on the back. He walked his newly found friend to the door.

Damien turned one last time. He'd wanted to leave a message for Delilah.

"Oh! If . . . *when* my wife returns, t-tell her I'm at the Misty Heights Hotel, over on Cedar Street, Room 153."

Before opening the door, he turned and said to his cohort.

"Oh, and tell her . . . I don't mind waiting." Then he stepped out the door.

Donnie leaned against the closed door for a minute or two. He had much to ponder in his heart regarding his own Christian walk.

"Today has truly been a good, good day!"

Chapter Eighteen

The smooth humming of the restored vintage Trans Am was abruptly interrupted by the booming sounds of an approaching car. Josh sat at a stop light on a one way street. The black Camaro pulled alongside him.

Anchored securely in the car's backseat were blaring speakers with decibels that reached ear shattering proportion.

Josh's cherished Trans Am vibrated with every pulsating beat of the obtrusive machine idling alongside it.

Josh quickly looked away after nodding to the car's occupants.

The sound of the revving engine prompted him to look once again.

The driver's thick black hair bounced with every movement of his head as he bobbed to every pounding beat.

"Do you want to race?" The driver mouthed to Josh.

The mean machine rocked to and fro, as the driver simultaneously pressed the gas pedal, then the clutch. The supped up vehicle's engine revved even louder.

Not only was the loudness coming from the car, but Josh thought the occupants to be a little unnerving, as well.

He thought he heard a few well-placed expletives coming

from the young men, but chose not to acknowledge or accept their challenge. He sped off as soon as the light turned green.

The other car's occupants used this as a challenge and sped up beside him. This time their look was more menacing.

The Trans Am slid easily into a lower gear leaving the challenger in the dust once again. But, true to form, the spurned Camaro caught up to him and now the two power-horses were neck to neck.

The unsolicited drag race had become frustrating to the Trans Am's driver. Just as he looked over to confront the agitators, he came face-to-face with the barrel of a .357 Magnum.

The hand gun was lowered out the window towards him, just as a shot rang out. The culprits then raced off, bowled over with laughter without bothering to see if, or what they'd hit.

Josh felt the blood trickling down his face and tasted the salty liquid in his mouth. He shakily pulled over to the curb to see what damage had been done to him, as well as his cherished chariot. As he stepped from the vehicle on wobbly legs, he fell backward and allowed the car to support his shaking body. A bystander ran over and inquired of his well-being.

"Are you alright, man?" The concerned gentleman who'd rushed to his aid asked. "You've been hit, you need a doctor. I'll call for one."

"N-No, but thanks, it's not necessary. I'm fine, I don't think I've been shot; just a little shaken is all."

"Well, you do have a nasty cut on your forehead." It's probably from flying glass, but I don't see any other damage. Thank God."

"Here, put this on your forehead."

The gentlemen, dressed in all white offered up his handkerchief to the injured victim.

"This should stem the bleeding. Let's get you over to this bench."

"You don't want to do that." Josh said. He focused fully on the stranger. "I might get . . . blood all over that white suit of yours."

"Oh, I'm not worried about that." The stranger said. "The important thing is to get you saved."

"Get me what?"

The moment the 'anointed' white cloth touched Josh's head, the flow of blood ceased. He felt as he did before the shooting incident, but was somewhat puzzled.

"Who are you?" He asked the man.

"I'm Master Prophet Eli Cummings." He took the handkerchief from the injured man's face. It had become pristine white once again.

What da?" Josh exclaimed. "Am I dreaming or am I dead? Either way, I'm getting away from here."

He began to rise, but his legs felt as if they were made of rubber. He sat quietly, mulling his close call over in his mind.

"You were wondering why those young men would do such a thing, when you hadn't even provoked them. Yet they wanted to kill you."

"As a matter of fact I was . . . and how d-did . . . ?"

He hadn't bothered to finish his question. Josh had already sensed the encounter was going to be anything but ordinary.

"I hadn't bargained to get my head almost blown off today."

"To calm your troubling mind, those young men were only doing what they knew to do.

You were merely a target to fulfill their master's desire. "The enemy only comes but to kill, to steal, and to destroy. "I'm sure you've heard that scripture before haven't you?"

"Uh, no, I-I haven't."

The all-knowing prophet knew this, but he'd asked the question to get the young man thinking; to do a little soul searching. The stranger sat quietly and watched closely as the young man sorted out his thoughts.

"I, uh, my wife that is . . . Tonika, goes to church with our neighbor, but I somehow never found my way to do so."

A crippling pang of remorse shot through his chest, at just the mention of her name.

A muted buzzing sound inside his pants pocket was heard at that moment. Josh pulled out his cell phone and read a text that had come in from his wife.

"Umph! That's strange . . . she wants to talk." Josh said in the air. "Wonder what that's all about."

"You would do well to oblige her." The prophet said. "After all, she is the victim here."

Josh sat shaking, as tears began to stream down his cheeks. He had wrestled with the decision all night long as he lay on the couch, while his wife lay sobbing in their bedroom.

What had kept him from going to her?" He wondered. He'd wanted to; to hold, to comfort and to ask for her forgiveness?

Maybe it was pride, or just plain old pigheadedness, or, was it the fear of rejection?

"What had possessed him to throw away his family, to chase behind a Jezebel?" He wondered. His co-worker had warned him, but being hard headed, he hadn't listened.

Karla, as it turned out was only interested in wrecking homes. He had thought he would move in with her; thinking he would be readily welcomed.

Instead, the door had been slammed in his face once she knew his home life was in shambles.

"Oh, no honey! You're no good to me like this!" She had laughed in his face.

"I don't want a full time man. It's too much bother. That's why I make it a practice to only date married men."

Karla had grabbed him by his shirt collar and had pulled him towards her. She had devilishly whispered.

"I just wanted to see you when *I* wanted to see you, because *I* knew *I* could have you at any given time. And you my little puppy . . . always came running!"

He heard her next words as if she was saying them at that exact moment.

"Go home to your silly little *wife!* I've had my fill of you!"

Then she had laughed a wicked laugh. Josh swore he saw her eyes turn a bright red.

"How do you feel?" Prophet Cummings asked, bringing the man back in focus.

"I feel as if I've lost everything. I've lost my job, my home, my self-respect, as well as my . . . soul."

"And what about your wife . . . where does she come in? Then, there's Ashad, your son, who looked up to you as his father."

"C-Can you make me feel any worse?" Josh asked, cradling his head in his hands. He sat in that position for what seemed like an eternity, before he heard the words.

"You can be forgiven. All you have to do is ask. Just as this hankerchief symbolized; "though your sins are of crimson, His blood washes them white as snow."

Josh's head jerked up, welcoming the ray of hope he'd just heard.

"Oh? Do you think my family will forgive my foolishness, and take me back?" He sat on the edge of his seat.

"It would be so wonderful. Why . . . I would be the best damn husband . . . a-and father . . ."

"No doubt you would Josh Gibbons, but there's someone else you really need to speak with."

"Who?" He thought long and hard.

"Oh yes . . . that's right."

Josh dropped to his knees and bowed his head. He prayed a devout prayer of redemption and forgiveness.

When next he opened his eyes, Josh found himself alone. He had wanted to thank the stranger.

He felt a prompting in his spirit to say "Let the redeemed of the Lord say so!"

"So!" Josh shouted from the depths of his soul.

"I am redeemed!"

Chapter Nineteen

E tta Mae observed a lone figure out of the corner of her eye, running along the sidewalk.

"Look! That looks like my sister! But what is she doing?"

"Oh . . . that is Dee and she's carrying her shoes in her hands!"

Tonika peered around Etta Mae to get a better look. "And she's singing!"

"Well, isn't that something? When I left she was still napping, now here she is skipping down the sidewalk bare foot."

Etta Mae blew her horn and stopped the car in the middle of the street.

"That knutt's acting like she's seen Jesus!" Tonika added satirically.

"Yeah right! Now, that would be a first!" Etta Mae rolled down the window and yelled.

"Dee! Hey Dee!"

The lone figure abruptly stopped, thinking she'd heard her name called. She peered inquiringly at the car's occupants, the evening sun in her eyes made it difficult to see.

"Oh, hey Sissy, guess what!"

She said breathlessly running up to the car.

"You're not going to believe . . . . Dee said taking a deep swallow.

"Dee! Girl, what are you doing? And why are you out here with no shoes?"

"Sissy . . . you're not going to believe who I spent the afternoon with!" It was all Delilah could do to try and contain her joy." Go on guess!"

The muscles in her face ached from all the smiling she'd done. She was filled with so much joy, so much peace and so much happiness.

Dee danced in place, and even twirled around, unable to contain her enthusiasm as she waited for her sister's response.

"Let's just amuse her." Etta Mae said to her passenger.

"Oh . . . I don't know . . . Jesus maybe?"

"*How did you know?*" Dee excitedly screamed. "Yes, yes, yes! And I met Him at the Well!"

"*You what . . .* what well? Girl, this ain't no time to be lying!" Her sister yelled. "Don't play with me like that!"

"Honest! Sissy, I'm not lying." Dee said with more conviction than necessary.

"There was this church, o-only it wasn't a church, and the name of it was *Re-Dig the Wells.*"

"Girl, get in this car. You must have been in the sun too long!"

Etta Mae pressed the automatic door lock to unlock the back door. Dee slid in, luxuriating in the new car smell and the comfortable leather seats.

Even the unwelcomed presence of Tonika sitting in the front seat, wasn't enough to damper her spirit. Her morning's experience was just too exhilarating.

"Dee, you remember my friend and neighbor, Tonika Gibbons."

"Yes . . . hello."

"Hello Delilah, good to see you again, it's been awhile."

"Girl, where are you coming from this time of the day?"

Etta Mae reached back to feel her sister's forehead.

"Ooh! You do feel warm. I sure hope you're not having a heat stroke!"

"No, I'm not having a heat stroke."

She welcomed the cool comfort of the vehicle, and allowed her tired frame to fall backwards.

"Why would you think that?"

Etta Mae turned to her friend. "Tonika! What did you just hear my sister say before she got in the car?"

"She said—

"She said she just saw Jesus, didn't she?"

Etta Mae focused her attention in the back seat through the rear view mirror.

"Now does that sound like someone coherent to you, Miss Dee? You; a devout agnostic saw the Lord?"

"But I did! I did see Him . . ." She was a bit subdued by her sister's unbelief.

"Well, now Etta Mae, she could have you know." This time, Tonika spoke up. "Look what's been happening to us all day, starting with this morning."

"Oh My God! Toni!" Etta Mae yelled, gulping a deep breath. "You're so right!"

Armed with that bit of revelation, the elated believer turned in her seat to address her sister.

"Dee! Delilah Collins! I do believe you! My God can do anything, anything He wants to do, because He is sovereign. Praise the Lord, Hallelujah!"

A warm glow crept from Etta Mae's neck up to her tear stained face.

"*My God!* My agnostic sister, of all people had a glorious Jesus encounter!"

"He can and will show Himself to anybody!" Tonika interjected, feeling a sense of elation herself. "And like you said, He is sovereign!"

The atmosphere inside the car had become an arena of praise. Unbridled tears flowed unashamedly, accompanied by thank you, Lord.

Tonika and Delilah rocked back and forth, and called on the name of Jesus.

Etta Mae broke into a prayer of thanksgiving.

"Heavenly Father, I thank you! Thank you! I don't know how, or what you did to my sister, but I thank you for saving her. Lord! I knew your Spirit was always within her. Father, you've always been with us, through all our ups and downs. And I'm glad you didn't give up on her. You were there all the time! Again, I just want to say thank you, Daddy! Thank you for honoring my grandmother's dying wish. Now, we've all come into the full knowledge of who *You* are.

Lord . . . hallelujah! Your child . . . my sister . . . Delilah! She has come home! Oh, hallelujah! Thank ya Je-sus!"

A blaring horn soon brought the afternoon praise-a-thon to a brazen halt.

The angry driver abruptly jerked his car past and menacingly glared at the car's occupants before speeding past.

Etta Mae composed herself and wiped the tears from her face with the back of her hand. The car eased forward as soft sobs were heard as she drove on.

The mellifluous presence of the Holy Spirit surrounded each of them.

"Etta Mae, I have to tell you all about my morning walk when we get home."

"I don't have the strength right now, but, my Lord! Umph, umph, umph!"

"I feel ya sistah. And He didn't do it without us!" Tonika glanced back at Dee.

"He didn't do what without you?"

Dee was unaccustomed to the neighbor's show of familiarity.

"Me and your sister said to the Lord; we said whatever He was doing to please don't do it without us."

"Yes! That's right, we did, didn't we? Dee, He allowed us to celebrate your deliverance."

Etta Mae's phone rang once again. She had left it lying on the seat next to her after she'd talked with Cynthia earlier.

"Hello, praise the Lord! Hi, hun, we're on our way home now. In fact, I'm turning onto the street as we speak."

Etta Mae listened as Donnie gave instructions for her sister.

"Damien was there, and wants Dee to meet him at the Misty Heights Hotel, you say?"

She glanced in the rear view mirror to gauge Dee's reaction to what was being said.

"What room is he in?" Dee wanted to know. "I'll talk to him. I can see clearly now."

"What room, honey?"

Etta Mae dared not pass judgment.

"Room 153 . . . O-okay . . . I'll turn around and take her there now. Yes, you're right, she does owe him that much."

Tonika couldn't help but overhear the conversation. It seemed as if a sense of compassion had occurred. Both Dee and her husband were now ready to hear each other out.

"Will wonders never cease?"

She said under her breath. The call brought her mind back to her plight. She too, was in need of mending.

"What about me Lord? Don't forget about me."

Just at that moment, her cell phone rang. It was her husband on the other end.

"H-hello . . . Josh . . . What? Are you there now?" Tonika's heart pounded. "You do? Uh huh."

She searched for Etta Mae's hand for encouragement. Then her face lit up with the biggest smile. Etta Mae gave the trembling hand a reassuring squeeze.

"I tell you what, I'll be there when you get . . . we're near home, but Etta Mae has to do a 'U' turn."

Tonika covered the mouth piece and exhaled a deep breath.

"Uh, huh." She interjected.

"You know what; it's not that far, so I can just walk home from here. I'll meet you there. O-okay, see you then."

"Eeeeeeee! He wants to talk!"

She yelled excitedly and grabbed her friend for a big hug. The elated woman was overcome with an indescribable peace.

"Etta Mae!" Tonika excitedly said. "Girl, let me off, I'll walk home from here."

She reached for the door handle even before the car had fully stopped.

"Wait, dunce! Let me stop the car first!"

The car rolled to a stop and the exuberant wife jumped out.

"Etta Mae, we have a lot to talk about. I'll see you tomorrow after church to feel you in. Okay?"

"See ya girlie, now get to stepping. Get home to your husband!"

The back seat passenger heard the exchange, and felt as if Tonika had usurped her sister's attention.

She desperately wanted Etta Mae's undivided attention tomorrow for herself. They also had much to talk about.

Tonika stepped up on the curb, then leaned down, peered into the window and shouted again.

"God is a good God! Amen?"

"Amen girlfriend." Etta Mae shouted back. "He's a restorer of anything the enemy has stolen away!"

Dee had gotten out of the back seat, fully intent on sitting in the front with her sister.

"Good-bye . . . Delilah." Tonika hesitantly said. She felt a kindred spirit with the delivered woman. Tonika sensed her friend's sister was close to getting her married life restored also.

She was unable to contain the excitement she was feeling and reached out and hugged the unsuspecting woman on a whim.

Dee was taken aback by the sudden affectionate gesture. She allowed herself to relax as seemingly, something appeared to have melted in her heart.

"Bye . . . fr-friend."

Just by saying those two little words, Dee was liberated from a jealous spirit. She now felt open to sharing her Etta Mae with her new friend, Tonika.

The woman had shown her nothing but kindness now, and when she had last visited. There was no reason she couldn't be friends with her sister's best bud, also.

The two held one another, and cried on each other's shoulders. The liberating feeling was just that overwhelming. Finally, they each stepped back. Dee, the first to speak, said to her sister in spirit.

"Friendship that flows from the heart cannot be frozen by adversity . . ."

"As the water that flows from the spring cannot congeal in

winter." Tonika said, finishing her newly acquired confidante's words.

"Thank you, James Fenimore Cooper!" Dee shouted.

"Thank you Jesus! They both shouted simultaneously.